FALL OF HOUSTON SERIES BOOK FOUR

NO SURRENDER

T.L. PAYNE

NO SURRENDER
Fall of Houston Series, Book Four

Copyright © 2021 by T. L. Payne
All rights reserved.

Cover design by Deranged Doctor Design
Edited by Melanie Underwood

Don't forget to sign up for my spam-free newsletter at www.tlpayne.com to be among the first to know of new releases, giveaways, and special offers.

Check out other books by T. L. Payne

Fall of Houston Series
No Way Out
No Other Choice
No Turning Back
No Surrender
No Man's Land (Pre-Order Now!)

The Days of Want Series
Turbulent
Hunted
Turmoil
Uprising
Upheaval
Mayhem
Defiance (Coming Summer 2021)

The Gateway to Chaos Series
Seeking Safety
Seeking Refuge

Seeking Justice
Seeking Hope

Although much of this story takes place in and around southern Louisiana, some aspects and locations have been altered to enhance the story. Many of locations are fictional. Thank you for understanding an author's creative license.

“Louisiana in September was like an obscene phone call from nature. The air - moist, sultry, secretive, and far from fresh - felt as if it were being exhaled into one's face. Sometimes it even sounded like heavy breathing.” — *Tom Robbins*

❀ Created with Vellum

Contents

Prologue   1
1. Will   9
2. Will   16
3. Will   24
4. Savanah   29
5. Savanah   36
6. Isabella   42
7. Will   48
8. Will   54
9. Walker   58
10. Savanah   66
11. Will   70
12. Isabella   76
13. Will   81
14. Will   88
15. Will   94
16. Savanah   100
17. Will   108
18. Isabella   118
19. Savanah   124
20. Will   132
21. Isabella   137
22. Savanah   141
23. Will   150
24. Savanah   157
25. Isabella   166
26. Isabella   173
27. Will   177
28. Will   183
29. Savanah   191
30. Will   196

Also by T. L. Payne 205
About the Author 207

Prologue

Fort Hood Army Base
  Killeen, Texas
  Event + Two Months

Analyst Rachel Stephens once again found herself sitting across the table from Brad Smith. The man was like a bad itch she just couldn't get rid of. She could think of no one with whom she would less like to be stuck in the apocalypse. And this situation certainly felt apocalyptic. In the two months since enemies of the United States had unleashed their weapons of war upon the nation, Stephens had witnessed the absolute worst things imaginable. She was deeply disturbed by the depths men sank to when faced with starvation and desperation.

When she'd first arrived at Fort Hood Army Base in central Texas after fleeing Houston following the deadly attack on Ellington Field Joint Reserve Base, Stephens had attended every meeting she was allowed and consumed every briefing about the state of the nation with hopes of finding a way of stopping something—anything. The daily reports about the death and destruction as the US military fought to hold off the Chinese incursion on American soil were nothing compared to the toll hunger, violence, injury, and disease were taking on the general population.

A balding man dressed in a wrinkled polo shirt and slacks spoke. "The experts' projection stating nine out of ten people will die within the first year in a total grid-down scenario appears to be all too accurate. Already, many cities are in ruins due to the looting and fighting over the few precious resources on store shelves and in warehouses. There are horrendous reports of large bands of people roaming the streets going from house to house scavenging, pillaging, and burning people out of their homes."

Stephens felt sick after each briefing, and once she determined that her expertise was not needed in any of the meetings, she stopped going. What good purpose did they serve? They could prevent none of it. Unless supplies could reach those cities, soon they'd all be wastelands left to a few murderous souls. She'd even at times found herself wondering why the military continued to fight off the Chinese and Russians along its shores. What was left to save at this point? She was feeling despondent. Hopelessness seeped into her every pore which wasn't in her nature. She'd always looked for a way to make the world a better place. And now, what could she do?

And then word came from the north by way of a single-engine plane, much like the one that had carried her from Houston to Fort Hood. With it came the first glimpse of the kingdom that General Walter Dempsey was creating for himself up in Illinois and the Midwest—everywhere, except Missouri, where somehow they'd managed to hold him back.

What a fool. Did he really think that the Russians and Chinese were going to let him keep it—even run it after they took the country? Stephens set her sights on him—on stopping him. That was something she could do. Not alone, of course, but she had the skill set to gather intelligence on his operation and find its vulnerabilities. If she could convince the commander to give her a team—or two—she could go there and find their supply chain and reroute it to the people who desperately needed it. There was still something she could do. And by hell, she was going to do everything she could—even if it only helped one community survive this damn thing, it would make it all worthwhile.

So, Stephens put her big girl panties back on and strode right into the daily briefing. She slicked her brown hair back and stuck an errant strand into its bun, slid into a chair across from Brad 'The Cad', and listened. She'd watch for an opportunity to speak with Waltrip about her plan.

Lieutenant General Robert Waltrip sat at the end of the table, his head buried in papers. The cables from the delegation of United States Congressmen who'd been in El Salvador when the event happened had asked for a report from the front lines.

Front lines? There'd been no lines. It had appeared to be more like a free-for-all for a while. China's ease at getting the Dongfeng armored vehicles ashore had been a surprise, but the US exploited the vehicles' weaknesses and shoddy construction, quickly taking out many of them. That led to the discovery of China's weakness—its corrupted manufacturing system.

"The PLA's Dongfeng is no match for our new Armored Multi-purpose Vehicle. The rumors of the poor-quality construction of the Dongfeng have proven true. There are reports of civilians breaking out the windows with baseball bats."

"Reports?" Waltrip asked. "Confirmed?"

"Yes, sir."

It seemed the elite troops were better equipped, but the rest of their force was stuck with faulty equipment and weaponry. Though they did have the advantage of communication and coordination, which the US lacked at the time.

That imbalance left the US at a significant disadvantage until the retaliatory strikes took out the power grids of both the Russian and Chinese and lessened their governments' effectiveness, inhibiting their communications with their ships at sea. The nuclear strike seemed to have little effect, in Stephens' view. They would have expected it—prepared for it. But the attack on their satellites had done the trick it seemed—thanks to the newly established Space Force and the secret missions outfitting civilian satellites with military capabilities. Now, they were as hampered communicating with their forces as the US was with its. Otherwise, there would be Russian and Chinese boots trampling on Dempsey's little kingdom by now. China had relied too heavily on their new naval fleet being able to penetrate and work effectively in and around the gulf coast and in the Atlantic. Now that communications had been cut off, the US saw significant gains in repelling the invasion.

After two months of holding off a complete invasion of the gulf coast, the US military found itself short on fuel, supplies, ammunition, and, most importantly, personnel. They were just spread too thin. Getting supplies to the front lines took too long, and medical help was too far away.

Waltrip ran a hand across the top of his freshly cut salt and pepper hair and glared around the table. "Why are our recruitment goals continually not being met?"

"No one wants to leave their families behind to starve or become victims to bandits," said a pretty, petite woman seated in the middle of the long conference table. She was dressed in uniform and surprisingly clean and well-groomed, considering their shower regime had been cut back to once per week. "Without a way of assuring people that their kids will not be left orphans in the streets, we can forget about parents."

"What happened to the draft? Why aren't we gathering people up and sending them south?" asked the short, stocky man next to her.

She twisted in her seat so that their eyes met. Her head turned slightly in a "you've got to be kidding" gesture. Stephens liked her. "First, when they see Humvees and military transport vehicles rolling into town, they run. They hide. We'd have to expend countless hours and manpower going from door to door searching for them and then wrenching them from their crying children's arms to throw them inside the transport trucks, guard them all the way there to make sure they didn't desert in order to get back to said children and then threaten to shoot them if they did not fight for the country that had made their children destitute on the streets." She turned back to face the group. "Is that the draft you were referring to?"

The man huffed as if he disagreed with her assessment of what was occurring.

"Why aren't these folks going to the shelters we've set up?" a middle-aged man dressed in a dingy white button-down shirt asked.

The woman pursed her lips. "They're scared. People, especially young, strong, and capable men, have been disappearing from those same shelters. Or so the rumors go." She turned her gaze toward the head of the table. Waltrip's aide looked up from the pile of papers on the desk in front of him. The woman raised one knowing eyebrow.

She was in the know. She was someone Stephens needed to talk to about Dempsey. Stephens felt encouraged for the first time in weeks. This woman had contacts with people off the base. From her tone and attitude, Stephens felt reasonably confident that she shared her view on how this war could be won. If not, it was likely she could convince her. Dempsey was the key. Stephens was sure of that one thing. He had the supplies and manpower to turn this whole thing around. The report was clear. He'd taken control of all the FEMA supplies in Region Five and commandeered the military in those states to secure them. He'd used Department of Homeland Security personnel to seize food, fuel, medical supplies, and other vital resources from communities under the guise of redistributing it to those who needed it but had instead stuck the supplies into underground warehouses for his own purposes. The news about work camps had disturbed Stephens the most. Citizens were being forced into labor camps to feed themselves and their families. The supplies originally intended for them were instead used to keep them captive. Although the news of forced labor camps where even small children were made to work rocked her to the core, but the thought of people still being alive gave her hope.

Americans were a resilient and patriotic nation. Suppose she could somehow manage to get the resources to care for families. People would step up to fight to protect them. Just as brave men and women had done during all significant conflicts throughout its history, the people of the United States would heed the call and defend their homeland. After—they'd work together to rebuild it. It was as simple and true as that. She just needed to get those resources and get them to the people—how hard could that be? Stephens sighed deeply. She'd need things like weapons, trucks, fuel. She'd also need people—trained and highly skilled people. She lifted her eyes to Waltrip and then to the woman. If it were possible—Stephens would find a way.

She stood and stretched her neck as Waltrip ended the meeting. Brad 'The Cad', of course, rushed around the table toward her. She held him off with an upraised palm. "I need to catch her," she said, pointing to the woman, and she headed toward the door. "Ma'am," Stephens said as she approached her. She stopped, stepped to one side to let others behind her pass, and turned to face Stephens. She stood five feet nothing in her flat-soled shoes. Dynamite came in small packages, and Stephens hoped she could use this one to blow up Dempsey's operation.

"I'm Analyst Rachel Stephens," she said with an outstretched hand. She glanced at the woman's name tape.

Williams. Colonel Williams.

"The analyst Stephens who brought us the encrypted disk from the Chinese consulate in Houston?"

Stephens blinked and bobbed her head once in acknowledgment. This woman was in the know.

"What can I help you with, Analyst Stephens?"

"That was what I wanted to talk to you about, ma'am. I'd like to run something by you that I think you might be able to help me with." She felt a queasiness in her stomach. She was nervous. Why? The woman just stared at her for a long moment, and Stephens' uneasiness grew. Was it hope? Was that what she was afraid of now? She hadn't yet resigned herself to the downfall of the nation or their freedom as a people. No matter how impossible the task ahead may seem, she was determined to pursue it—no matter the risk. And no matter who she had to align herself with.

Brad slid in beside her. She cast him a dirty look, but he pretended to ignore her gesture. Williams checked her watch. It was a classic, timelessly elegant piece and looked antique. "Let's move this into my office. I have a few moments before my next meeting."

Stephens stepped around Brad to follow Williams. "I'll catch you up at lunch."

Brad huffed and started to follow them through the door.

"Don't you have a meeting of your own to attend, Mr. Smith?" Williams asked. There was something more than dismissal in her tone. They knew each other. It figured. Brad 'The Cad' strikes again.

ONE

Will

Event + Two Months

In the relative silence created by the lack of man-made noise, Will could hear the roar of an engine for several minutes before the all-terrain vehicle and its rider came into view. Will aimed his rifle's sight on the rider's torso, his finger moved inside the trigger guard, and he exhaled, ready to take the shot.

"It's Corey," Isabella said, lowering the monocular she held to one eye.

Will inhaled, taking in a deep breath, and blew it out. It was no small thing, taking another man's life. He was grateful he would be able to avoid it this time. In the weeks since arriving in Calcasieu Parish, he'd had been forced to kill at least a half dozen times. Any notion that he'd enjoy life at leisure once he arrived at his sister's place had quickly been set aside.

The rider stopped the quad in the middle of the road, removed her helmet, and shook her head before pushing a mass of curls from her attractive face. Isabella stood and stepped out from their ground hunting blind. She'd raised her hand to wave Corey over when the shot rang out. Will dove for Isabella, knocking her to the ground, and the two crawled back to the blind and began scanning the woodline, trying to determine where the shooter was.

"Where's Corey?" Isabella asked as she peered through the monocular.

Will scanned the gully to the left of the quad. "She made it. She's in the gully."

"Found them," Isabella said. "I've got one shooter at our ten o'clock about six hundred yards."

Will shifted and spotted the shooter right where Isabella had said he was, but he was too concealed for a clean shot, and Will was not about to waste ammunition. He turned his attention back to Corey. She was moving slowly north, doing her best to remain low. As she drew closer to their position and the point where she'd need to leave the ditch, Will called out to her. "Make it quick, Corey. I'll cover you." As Corey climbed out, he lifted his AR-15 and fired in the direction of the shooter. In seconds, Corey dove and rolled inside the well-concealed blind.

"A little heads-up would have been nice!" Corey spat as she scrambled to her feet.

"Heads-up? We've been sitting here for hours and didn't know he was there," Isabella said, helping her brush weeds from her auburn hair.

"Those bastards are like freaking cockroaches," Corey said. "I came up to tell you guys that the military is pulling back this way. We'd been hearing bombing for two days before the first convoy came through. There's heavy fighting not more than ten miles from us."

Isabella gasped, and her hand rose to her throat. "That close!"

"The soldiers that I talked to said not to worry. They were just moving their headquarters and supplies. They were confident that they would be able to defeat them soon."

"How many are there?" Isabella asked, her voice pitchy.

"They wouldn't give details, but Dad sent some guys down to

see if we needed to prepare to bug out, and they said there were a shit ton of Chinese fighters and tanks just south of the airport. Somebody blew holes all along the runway. Ain't nobody landing any planes there."

Isabella turned to Will. "They're too close." Tears glistened in her eyes. Her fear was understandable. They'd seen firsthand the damage a few hundred insurgents could do. An army with tanks and proper military weapons would be far worse.

"What's your dad's plan?" Will asked Corey.

"He left two guys down there. If they cross Highway 108, we're all heading this way."

Isabella's forehead furrowed, and she touched Will's arm. "How far away is that?"

"Twenty or so miles."

"Gawd!" She bent over at the waist and sucked in a deep breath.

"They're moving really slow, and the military is still between them and us," Corey said.

"If the military can't defeat them, what chance do we have?"

"They're waiting for reinforcements, or so the dude I spoke to said. The National Guard from Arkansas is even headed this way."

"What the hell is taking them so long?" Isabella asked.

"Lack of technology would be my best guess." Corey nodded toward the woodline where the shooter was located. "What are we going to do about him?"

Will raised his rifle and peered through the scope. He scanned from right to left until he spotted Walker's blind. If he hadn't known right where to look, he would have never seen it. "Walker and Tank will take care of him." Isabella had expressed some concern when his cousins and their crew from the casino in Vincent had agreed to join forces to defend their community. She'd since come to learn that although their outfit liked to play hard, they were just down-to-earth and fiercely patriotic folks, people with families. When they'd learned who was behind the EMP and that foreign invaders had dared step on Cajun soil, they'd immediately set to work devising a plan to secure the area. The well-concealed hunting blinds had been Troy's idea. Nearly thirty people now guarded their southern border along the various rain-swollen gullies and bayous at least two miles from their homes along Sugar Cove Road.

Will continued scanning low to the ground. Walker and Tank were impossible to see in the brush. He waited for movement. A second later, the grass moved ever so slightly. "They're making their way there now."

As the three of them waited for the sound of gunfire to tell them Walker and Tank had acquired their target, Will rehearsed their bug-out plan over and over in his mind. The group had grown since Will and the others had arrived. Savanah's pastures were now filled with tents and motor homes where, in addition to Tank's crew, some of the neighbors who'd been made aware of the battle raging thirty miles to their south had opted to move closer to the protection of the new Sugar Cove security force. Even with all the extra armed patrols, Will still was unable to relax.

They wouldn't have much time to flee. Everyone had been instructed to have a go-bag packed with the barest of essentials ready to go at a moment's notice. They'd be going on foot. The military had taken all available fuel in town, and running the four-wheelers and side-by-sides up and down the roads doing patrols and manning observation posts had used up most of their gasoline.

Boom!

"One shot. One kill," Will said under his breath. They were low on ammo and couldn't afford to do any target practice. Walker had taken over responsibility for weapons training. Five rounds were all a new shooter was afforded to practice with—certainly not enough to be proficient. Hopefully, they wouldn't need to be. Those that had never handled a weapon before were assigned to the rear, where they would be the last line of defense—if it came to that. Will was determined that it wouldn't, which meant that he'd taken double shifts and was operating on only a few hours of sleep a day. They all were running on empty.

The Chinese weren't their only threat. The remaining Blanchards had been full of bluster in the days following the battle in Vincent that had left Buzz and his henchmen dead. After the military rolled through town, Valson had escaped, along with several of his relatives. They'd waited a week or more before returning to Sugar Hill and attempting to ramp up their previous efforts to terrorize and plunder their way through the parish.

"You think they got him?" Isabella said, pulling Will from his thoughts.

"Yeah. There would have been a lot more shooting if they hadn't."

Will hadn't wanted Isabella to join the watch teams. He'd tried to convince her to stay behind, to guard the farm and the children, but she'd have none of that. When Walker had tried to put her on a different shift from Will, she'd balked, even when Walker said he'd be her partner. She'd made out that it was the only time they had to be alone together, but Will suspected it was something more. He thought maybe she was concerned that he'd take unnecessary risks without her there to remind him that he was still Cayden's only parent. He didn't need her to remind him of that. But things were different now. He had family there to rely on in case he didn't return, so maybe she was right though, in some ways, it was harder having her there with him. His concern for her safety might put others at risk. He didn't want to make that mistake.

A moment later, Tank appeared in the open field, holding his thumb into the air.

"They got him," Will said. "I'll be right back."

~

Will met Tank near the large row of blackberry bushes the shooter had been hiding behind. "Is he local?" Tank knew what he meant by that. The man was dressed in hunter's camouflage, and his face was painted black and green. It was hard to tell his nationality. Will's eyes landed on his rifle, leaning against a nearby tree. Walker picked it up and stared through its scope.

"That looks expensive."

"It probably was," Walker replied.

"He ain't Chinese. He could be local, but I don't know him. He was obviously waiting to take out our messengers though. He fired as soon as Corey stopped," Tank said.

"Did you check his pockets?" Isabella asked as she walked up behind them. "He could be carrying a wallet or some form of identification."

Tank nodded toward the man on the ground. "Help yourself."

Isabella approached the dead man and stood over his body. She studied him for a moment before kneeling and rolling him onto his side. Will rushed over and held him as she reached into his back pocket. "He's not Chinese. His driver's license says he's from Bethesda, Maryland."

Tank's eyebrows raised. "Maryland?"

"That's a suburb of Washington, DC," Will said.

"What's he doing down here? And why is he shooting at our messengers?" Isabella asked. She pulled a business card from his wallet, stared at it for a moment, and handed it to Will whose eyes grew wide. "Wasn't he Kim Yang's handler?"

"Who's Kim Yang?" Corey asked as she approached them.

"She was a Chinese spy we met in Houston," Isabella said.

Corey held both hands up, palms out, and took a step back. "Wait a minute. What's going on here?"

Will shook his head. "I have no idea." None of it made sense to him. How this shooter was related to Kim Yang and the men she worked with, Will didn't know, but his presence there sent up about a million red flags. "We need to alert someone."

"The military convoy should be through here in a few hours. Maybe you should tell them."

"Maybe they were his target," Isabella said.

"Then why the hell did they shoot at me? I don't look like a soldier," Corey said.

"Probably just passing the time with a little target practice," Tank said, picking up the rifle and inspecting it for himself.

$\sim$

When the military convoy rolled through on its way south toward the front lines, the lieutenant that Will spoke to didn't seem to understand the significance of finding the business card of a Chinese spy in the pocket of the dead shooter.

"I'll pass this information on to my command," was the extent of the man's reply. He looked bone-weary. The fighting and the pressure to hold the enemy back from the interior of the country must have been an enormous weight on all the soldiers.

"I have to get back. My dad will want to know what happened here today," Corey said, throwing a leg back over her quad and starting the machine. "We'll send word if they cross the highway."

Will was determined to be ready to leave whether that occurred or not. He'd just have to convince the others that it was the wisest course of action.

TWO

Will

In the days since Corey had brought news that the fighting was nearing Highway 108, Will was always on edge, waiting for the day the war spilled over into their world. Will had been even more vigilant pulling more and more watch shifts. He yawned as he slid his foot into his boot, pulled the laces tight, grabbed his pack and rifle, and walked toward the door. He glanced back at his sister, who was at the kitchen sink still in her bathrobe. The sun had just peeked over the horizon, but the farm was already alive with activity.

Isabella tilted her head to one side and placed a hand on her hip. "I thought all the guard shifts were already covered."

They were. But even though weeks had passed since the visit from Corey and they'd heard nothing more about the battle along the coast. It had been a little over two months since the world went dark, and Will was yet to feel any more settled into his new life at the homestead in Calcasieu Parish, Louisiana.

It seemed that the number of occupants kept growing as nearby residents either ran out of resources or fell victim to raiders. At some point in the last few weeks, Will had lost count of how many people had banded together on his sister's farm. They'd had to extend their borders to the Bertrands' property to accommodate all the RVs and hastily thrown-together shacks that the refugees now called home. The Bertrands were happy to return to their farmhouse and open their doors to them.

"I just need to go check on everyone—make sure they have all the ammo and supplies they need," Will said before shutting the door behind him.

He didn't wait for another lecture from Isabella or Savanah about him pushing himself too hard. They just didn't understand. The stakes were too high to trust all the details to strangers. Not when the safety of his family was at risk; he worried that they relied on old-world thinking, unaware of the magnitude of the dangers outside their community.

As he walked up the drive toward Sugar Cove Road, he passed Jason and Blake coming in after their shifts had ended. They gave one another curt nods and continued on their way. Will pulled up his T-shirt and wiped the sweat from his brow. It was turning out to be rather warm for mid-November, and Will already felt drained from the heat.

The day-to-day struggle to keep everyone fed and safe had taken its toll on them all. Nerves were frayed, and with everyone living in such close quarters, tensions were running high among the survivors of Sugar Cove Road. He and Jason had different ideas on how to go about ensuring that the residents of Sugar Hill were no longer a threat and remained behind their gates, Will being convinced that Jason's interest was in protecting his family members who may or may not be residing there. Will had wanted them all gone. They'd compromised by placing a checkpoint just outside the community's gate.

Will stepped through the gate and headed west.

"Dad?" Cayden called from the gate at the end of Savanah's driveway.

"Yeah, Cayden?"

"I can take a shift, and you could get some rest."

Will stopped in the middle of the road and looked back at his thirteen-year-old son. He seemed to have aged years since the day of the EMP, yet it was still difficult for Will to let go and stop treating him like a little boy. He had promised Melanie that he'd protect him, and he was doing everything he could to keep that promise.

"I'm good, son. I just need to check on things since Pete and Rob went to town."

They'd gone to speak with Will's cousins, Tank, Troy, and Gabby, to see what they'd learned from their visit to Fort Polk. He was anxious for news about the war with the Chinese that had so far managed to remain south of the Intercoastal Waterway.

"Can I just come with you to the roadblock? There's nothing else for me to do. Karson and I have already cleaned out the barn and fixed the hog's pen for today."

Will studied Cayden as he stood with his arms draped over the gate and a rifle slung over his back. Everyone went armed whenever they were outside of their homes. It was the rule. They'd had some skirmishes with the residents of Sugar Hill in the early days, and they weren't taking any chance of getting caught off guard.

The corners of Will's mouth curled up slightly. "Run and tell Isabella where you are going so she doesn't send out a search party."

"Wait right there," Cayden called over his shoulder as he ran back toward the old farmhouse.

Will knew Isabella would be pleased that they would be spending time together. She'd chastised Will several times about making it a priority, even though there was so much to do. He and Isabella were growing closer every day. She loved Cayden, and he adored her. It seemed wrong somehow to be falling in love when the whole world was going to shit around them, but Will couldn't help himself. Isabella was amazing and filled his life with hope in the midst of the darkness.

It seemed that the event had brought his sister love as well.

Will had strongly objected to her relationship with Jason Blanchard. The Jason he'd known was as bad as the rest of his family, but from what Will had witnessed since he'd arrived in Calcasieu Parish, Jason seemed to genuinely love Savanah and the kids, though Will wasn't convinced that he wasn't also loyal to his family.

The smile on Cayden's face as he ran back toward Will melted away the negative thoughts swirling in his brain about Jason and the rest of the Blanchards. It was so good to see Cayden happy for a change. They'd spent the prior two years in such a dark place after Cayden's mother had died, and although they'd faced unprecedented hardship since the EMP took out the power grid and sent the nation back to the Stone Age, Will's relationship with his son had never been better. In many ways, he believed he had Isabella to thank for that.

"What's that?" Will asked, pointing to the bundle in Cayden's right hand.

Cayden's smile spread from ear to ear. "Cookies."

"Oatmeal or peanut butter?"

"Oatmeal," Cayden replied. "With raisins. Savanah said you forgot to eat breakfast—again."

Finding enough food to feed everyone was getting harder and harder every day. Will knew that soon, they'd be heading into winter with nothing. He couldn't enjoy his bacon and eggs, knowing so many people were literally starving to death.

Cayden stuffed the cookies into a pouch on the side of his backpack and opened the gate. His grandfather's old tractor had been moved back to the barn after the threat of someone plowing through the gate on a motorized vehicle had been eliminated by the roadblocks at both ends of Sugar Cove Road and the booby traps along the drive had been removed to make it safe for all the newcomers and their children. Will looked back at the field where his grandfather used to have his horses. It was now filled with campers and tents.

"Let's get going and make our rounds," Will said as he shut the gate behind Cayden.

As they walked toward the Sugar Hill roadblock, Cayden asked, "When do you think Pete and Rob will get back and let us know what they're saying at the army base?"

It was all that had been on everyone's minds since Corey had described the fighting potentially crossing the Intercoastal Waterway. So far, the military from Fort Polk, along with National Guard units, had held their own against the invading Chinese army but the word was that they were running low on supplies, and moving more to the front lines was difficult due to the lack of transportation.

In addition to running low on munitions, they'd put a call out for all able-bodied residents to join the fight. That was when Will had known just how dire the situation was. He struggled with his decision to stay and protect his family over joining the battle and saving the nation. He struggled with it every day. His gaze fell upon his son. He'd promised Melanie he'd protect and care for him. They had been their last words to one another and he couldn't break that promise. If he died, who would protect his family?

As Will and Cayden approached the line of cars, trucks, and tractors that blocked the intersection near Sugar Hill's gated community, he spotted Jane and Luca standing close together whispering. Jane glanced up and then quickly looked away. Whatever they were discussing was obviously personal and private. He wouldn't pry by asking.

"What's wrong?" Cayden asked as they approached the couple.

"Wrong?" Luca said, avoiding their gaze. "Nothing's wrong. It's been very quiet in there for our entire shift."

Cayden looked up at Will with a questioning look. Will shook his head slightly, indicating that Cayden shouldn't push the matter.

"You have everything you need? Do you have enough water? You're keeping hydrated, right?" Will asked, turning to the reason for their visit to the roadblock.

"Yep," Jane said, slinging her rifle around to the front and returning to her lawn chair near the edge of the roadway.

The observation post had been situated three hundred yards from the gate, and they'd placed their lawn chairs in such a way as to position the SUV's big engine between the chairs and the front gate. The wrought-iron structure could be seen through the SUV's side glass and windshield. Others had positioned themselves in the beds of a few of the pickup trucks during their shifts. There were no hard and fast rules except to keep anyone from exiting that gate.

Will was aware that the residents could leave the community via the back of the property. He was fine with that. They had someone hidden on that side as well, monitoring who was coming and going. As of yet, none of the Blanchards had been spotted, a fact that did little to ease Will's mind. They could be anywhere. He knew that family well and they would not let the death of their patriarch and kin go unavenged. Sooner or later, they would attempt to exact their revenge. Will and the survivors at the farm could not afford to let their guards down. Besides, they weren't their only threat. In these desperate times, neighbors had turned on neighbors in the fight for food to feed their starving families. Other groups had formed—some better armed and trained than Will's—he knew it was only a matter of time before trouble reached them, either from bandits, the Blanchards, or the the invaders along the coast.

They were reasonably prepared for marauders and even the Blanchards, but there was no way to be prepared for an army with modern, sophisticated weaponry.

Will glanced over at Luca who still wore a guilty look. The kid had a terrible poker face. They'd been discussing leaving, Will imagined but may have felt some sense of duty to their community to stay and help protect and defend it.

Will nodded for Cayden to stand behind the big truck and approached Luca. "You and Jane thinking of going out on the next run?"

Luca stiffened and stuffed his hands into the front pockets of his skinny jeans.

He looked surprised and then relieved. "Yeah. We were thinking we might want to see for ourselves how things were out there. We haven't left the community since the lights went out. We thought we'd go with August's group when they go again."

"That would be good. We need a fresh pair of eyes on the situation regarding the refugees heading to Shreveport. I've heard rumors. I know that Savanah would feel better having fresh intelligence, just in case we have to bug out that way."

Luca's shoulders relaxed, and he removed his hands from his pockets then looked at Jane. "She's concerned about her family. She wants to find a way to get word to them that she's all right."

"I can understand that. What about your family?"

"My folks and brother are in Seattle. I doubt word would reach that far."

"I hear that the West Coast was spared. They say they even still have electricity."

"That's what Pete said. That came from some private at the base, though, so who knows. Rumors are rampant these days."

"That they are," Will said. "Still, it would be good to see first-hand about the route to Shreveport. August said he was going to move north and stay close to our proposed route looking for supplies. He plans to go as far as he can on the fuel he has left in that old truck Pete found last week ."

The truck had been found in an old barn covered in moving blankets. Someone had once been attempting to lovingly restore it. Pete was able to get it running by replacing the battery and everyone had been thrilled to learn it had a full tank of gas. They'd been saving it for the trip north. But there was no way it would carry everyone in their growing community, so it had been decided that August would use it to find supplies and do reconnaissance on alternative routes to Shreveport—those less traveled and less likely to have bandits waiting to ambush them.

"Hopefully, we'll come back with good news," Luca said.

Will nodded. His gaze turned to Cayden, who was scanning the Sugar Hill community's fence line through the scope of his rifle. The trip from Houston to Calcasieu Parish had almost cost them their lives multiple times. He did not want to be forced to take his son back out on the road regardless of the news the team brought back, but he needed to consider all their options and leave everything on the table.

THREE

Will

"Hey, Will."

Walker had appeared out of nowhere. Will chastised himself for not being more alert. The Texas Ranger could have just as easily been a foe rather than a friend. The lawman still wore his white western hat and white shirt and tie and Will wondered if he still carried his gold star in a wheel badge. The nickname that Monte had given him had stuck even after Monte had left to find his family down south along the Louisiana coast.

"Here," he said, holding out a thermos. "Isabella sent it. It's the real deal. That's one special girl you got there."

Will smiled. He agreed. He felt blessed but worried he might blow it with her. It was hard to balance everything.

"Any sign of you know who?" Walker asked, pointing toward the wrought-iron gate locking in the residents of Sugar Hill.

"Not yet. Tank and Troy think Valson and what was left of the Blanchards took off toward the east after their skirmish with the military. They have family living in Starks."

Walker leaned against a brand-new Jeep Grand Cherokee.

Will admired the vehicle and lamented that the shiny red SUV

24

was no more use than a hunk of metal and plastic. "You're not convinced?" Walker asked.

"Jason isn't and he knows them better than anyone. If he is still looking for them, then they are still around here somewhere."

Walker adjusted his hat, revealing more of his face. "Maybe it's just wishful thinking. Maybe he wants the closure of knowing whether his kin is dead or alive."

"Either way, we need to stay on guard. We can't afford to be blindsided by his vengeful relatives."

"Don't you think they'd go after your cousins and that outfit at the casino first? After all, he is the one that came to rescue you."

Will ran a hand across his stubbled chin. "They're all cowards when you get right down to it. They'll go after the easiest targets. Troy and Tank held them off for weeks before we arrived and upset their truce. The only way that happened was the Blanchards didn't want a bloodbath. They wanted easy victims like the elderly and unprepared residents out here."

"I agree that we should remain cautious, but there are other threats to guard against," Walker said.

Will unscrewed the lid to the thermos and took a drink. As the caffeine hit his bloodstream, he sighed in pleasure. It was a horrible addiction—caffeine. One that he'd be forced to abandon soon. He didn't imagine they'd be getting any shipments of coffee beans from Columbia for a very long time.

"We have to be ready for anything. It sucks that we can't do live-fire training so that folks can at least learn how to hit what they aim at."

"We just can't afford to use up the ammunition right now."

"I know." Will shifted from one foot to the other and looked south. "I just hope the military doesn't run out before they push General Yuen and his army back to China."

"They're doing all they can to keep the supply chain open. Insurgents blew up the railroad bridge at Lake Charles, but they were ready for them at the one in DeRidder. Oh, by the way, I forgot to tell you, I heard from Monte."

"What? When?" Will asked, turning to face Walker as he stroked his chiseled jawline.

"Late yesterday evening. One of the lookouts from Choupique sent word that they were heading this direction on their way to Shreveport. He finally convinced his wife's family to leave their camps and head to the refugee facility to wait this out."

"That's a relief—that they will be out from behind enemy lines, I mean."

"You don't think much of the refugee facilities?"

"I don't know. I think my opinion of government-run facilities is jaded by how they handled Hurricane Katrina and other natural disasters. They were even less prepared for the magnitude of the crisis at the Mexican border. I just think we need a solution that doesn't rely on the government, a long-term solution because things aren't going back to normal any time soon, even after we defeat the Chinese. All the infrastructure that has been destroyed will take many months, if not years, to rebuild. In the meantime, we have to find a way to survive."

"Your sister's homestead is pretty good, but—"

"I know. It's not sustainable. We need to be able to hunt and fish in addition to growing crops. There are just too many people vying for too few resources here. I bet the deer, rabbit, and squirrel population has already been cut in half."

"It sounds like you've been thinking a lot about the long term. Any ideas of a better place to go?"

"I was thinking Arkansas, maybe. It was less populated before things went to shit. The Ozarks were full of game. I hunted there with a buddy once up near Mountain Home. I thought we could spend some time at the facility in Texarkana and send out scouts to find a suitable area to settle in," Will said with a question in his tone. He hadn't told anyone else about his idea yet as they seemed so set on staying at the homestead.

"It sounds like a viable plan. I like the idea of having the FEMA facility as a safe base for everyone while we look. It would give us time to properly evaluate and investigate instead of feeling like we had to be in a hurry to pick a spot."

"That's what I was thinking too."

"The journey to Texarkana won't be easy," Walker said.

Will stared down at the pavement. He knew the dangers they'd face out on the road. What had been left unsaid was the challenge of convincing everyone to uproot and leave before things got too bad and while they were still healthy enough to make the trip. People underestimated the toll that malnutrition takes on a body. Will could feel it. He already moved slower and planned his activities during the day for when he had the most energy. The adults were sacrificing meals to make sure the children were well fed. He understood. He did the same with Cayden, but was it the wisest move? Who would take care of the little ones when the adults were too emaciated to find food or defend the homestead?

"When do you plan on having this conversation with the others?" Walker asked.

Will looked up. "I was hoping you'd join me in that one—maybe sit everyone down tomorrow after the midday meal?"

Walker removed his hat and wiped the sweat from his brow with a white handkerchief. "I can do that. Are you prepared for the push back?"

Will glanced over at Luca and Jane and then to Cayden. "There isn't any other option. We'll just have to make everyone see that. I suspect that there are others thinking something similar, but since we haven't had a meeting in weeks, no one has addressed it."

Walker stuffed his handkerchief into his back pocket and adjusted the hat back on his head. He lifted one eyebrow. "You ready to leave your family and go without them if they choose to stay?"

Will knew who he was talking about. He'd gone back and forth about it for weeks. Could he leave his sister and her children behind to save Isabella and Cayden? Truth be told, Savanah was the only reason Will was still in Calcasieu Parish. He just had to find a way to convince her that leaving was their only option— even if it meant leaving Jason behind. He prayed she'd see reason, unable to bear the alternative.

FOUR

Savanah

CALCASIEU PARISH, LOUISIANA

Event + Two Months

"Mom, Kylie has my tractor and won't give it back," Keegan yelled as he chased his sister through the outdoor kitchen where Savanah had once created her herbal teas and candles. Now it was where the community prepared meals for the forty or so people that now called her farm home.

Mrs. B stepped in front of Kylie and grabbed the toy. "How about you come to help me grind the wheat?"

"Aw—it's too hot inside. Jason said he'd take me swimming in the pond this afternoon," Kylie said, stomping her foot.

"Kylie," Savanah said. Kylie turned, and Kegan stuck out his tongue at her.

"Mom," she whined.

"Go inside and help Mrs. B. Jason will come for you when he is ready for a swim."

Kylie frowned and stomped off toward the house as Savanah continued. "She's right, Mrs. B. It is too hot to be inside today."

"I'm not going to stay in very long. I'm going to try to get her down for a nap. She'll be a lot less cranky, and I could use one myself."

"Thanks, Mrs. B—for everything."

Mrs. B smiled. She reminded Savanah so much of her grandmother. They were close in age and had the same kind and generous disposition. She was blessed to have Mrs. B as part of their new family.

"It's been a blessing being useful again," Mrs. B said as she turned to follow Kylie.

"Keegan, would you tell Luca that we're almost out of wood for the stove? We have another hour or so to go on dinner."

"Okay, Momma. Can I go play with my friends after?"

He and Kylie had been thrilled to have other children with whom to play. Some of their older neighbors had volunteered to corral and watch over them while the parents worked to keep the community safe and fed, but some of the kids still managed to find ways to get underfoot, mostly Kylie and Keegan. Karson had become Jason's shadow.

Savanah nodded, and Keegan ran off toward what had, just weeks before, been their back pasture. Now, it was lot C in their RV park. Jason, Luca, and her cousin Troy had been hauling Porta Johns in from a construction site near town. Four of them between the thirty or so people camping there wasn't enough, but it was something.

After Jane and Luca finished their shifts at the checkpoint, she'd come to help Savanah prepare dinner. Savanah was grateful for the help. "Jane, you mind stirring the stew? I want to check on Myrtle. She didn't eat when I fed the pig this morning."

Jane cut the greens from the top of a turnip and placed them in a bowl before standing. As she stepped toward the wood-fired stove, her hand flew up to cover her mouth, and she ran out the door. Savanah followed her, holding Jane's braids back as she vomited in the dirt.

"Are you all right?"

Jane wiped her mouth with the back of her hand and straightened. She was sweaty and pale. Savanah felt her forehead with the back of her hand. "You don't seem to have a fever."

"I don't think it's viral, Savanah." The corners of her lips curled up, and Savanah's eyes widened.

"Are you?"

Jane nodded as the color began returning to her cheeks. "I know it's awful timing. That's why Luca and I haven't said anything. With all that's going on and all."

Savanah placed her palm on Jane's flat stomach. "Are you kidding? This is wonderful news. In the midst of all this mess, a new life being brought into the world signals hope."

She hadn't known Jane but a few weeks, but they'd grown as close as sisters in that time. Having a baby in the group added a new dynamic, especially if they were forced to flee, but they'd all seen so much death and destruction that they needed to be reminded that the cycle of life continued, and they were fighting to make a better life not only for themselves but for future generations.

"You should get out of this heat and get some rest. Why don't you go on over to the pond and sit under the willow trees?"

Jane smiled. "Maybe just for a few minutes. I'll come back and get the rest of the turnips cut up in a bit."

"No, don't worry about that. Rob's wife is coming to make some fancy dish with roasted turnip with wilted greens. She'll finish up for you."

"Thanks for being so understanding, Savanah. I promise to still pull my weight around here." She glanced down at her stomach then looked up and scrunched her face. "I am not looking forward to getting as big as a house. Luca's mother said he weighed over eleven pounds when he was born."

"Ouch!"

"I know. I'm kinda scared about it."

"Don't worry. It's bad for the baby," Savanah said.

Savanah would do the worrying for the both of them. Giving birth without modern technology and medicine could prove fatal for Jane or the baby. Before the advancement of maternity and neonatal care, infant mortality was fairly high and the fact that someone could once again die from an infected cut due to the lack of antibiotics was always on her mind. They would have to make sure Jane received proper nutrition and monitor her closely to ensure a safe delivery and healthy baby.

As Savanah watched Jane head down to the pond, she worried again about the health of the rest of the community. They'd already used up most of her herbal remedies and store-bought medical supplies. What they really needed was a doctor and a fully stocked pharmacy. With the amount of manual labor involved in securing the farm, keeping people fed, and the dozens of other daily tasks, they'd seen an increasing number of injuries. Most were minor, but some were potentially life-threatening. It was just one of the million things that kept her awake at night.

"Keegan said you were out of wood," Jason called as he dropped an armload of wood into the box just outside the door.

"Thanks."

"My pleasure," Jason said, leaning in and giving her a peck on the cheek.

She half smiled and turned her gaze toward the pond. In the weeks following the shoot-out in town that had ended in his father's death, along with many other relatives, she and Jason had grown close. His father had taken her brother hostage and been killed by their cousin, Tank. That fact should have complicated their relationship, but it hadn't. They'd spoken at length about their families and in the end, they'd both agreed that you couldn't choose your parents.

Will was finally beginning to accept the relationship. After spending time with Jason on guard duty and working to secure the farm, they seemed to have put their differences aside. Savanah hoped that they would develop a friendship; she'd had no difficulty accepting Isabella and Savanah thought it was great that they'd found each other despite the chaos all their lives had become. And Cayden adored Isabella. It would all be so perfect if it weren't for the apocalypse—and war.

Savanah scanned the field where the goats were kept. "Where's Karson?"

"Helping Luca learn to shoot the crossbow."

Savanah smiled but inside, she didn't like that her ten-year-old son was growing up so fast. As the eldest son, he somehow felt he was the man of the house and needed to protect his family. She and Jason had spoken to him after they'd told the children they were growing close. Karson had been quiet for a long time after, but in many ways, he may have been relieved not to have to carry all the responsibility. She now believed that if she and Jason decided to marry and he moved into the house, Karson would be fine with it.

"I'm surprised he let you get away."

Jason picked up two sticks of wood with one hand and opened the door. "He looked quite proud of himself."

He was loading the wood into the stove when Savanah heard an engine and turned toward the road. Her pulse quickened, expecting the worst.

"It's Corey," Jason said, hurrying out the door and stepping into the middle of the driveway. He raised his hand to wave, and she stopped ten feet from them.

"What's up?" Savanah said, approaching her.

After Corey had filled them in on the battle between the US military and the Chinese south of Highway 108, Savanah paced back and forth across the driveway. It was becoming clearer by the moment that they were going to lose the farm. "It's too close. If they break through, they could be here before we could get everyone rounded up and far enough away," she said as she passed Jason.

He was staring off toward the gate, likely thinking the same thing. "We'll know more when Will and the others make it back. We can have a meeting and decide what our next steps need to be. Okay?" Jason stroked her arm. "Please don't give up hope yet."

Hope? How did one hold on to hope in such perilous times? Every time things started looking better, they would get the rug pulled out from under them.

"Will and Cayden made it home. They went through hell out there on the road, but they made it here. We'll make it too— together—all of us."

Mrs. B had led a crew of workers assembling makeshift tables so that everyone not on guard duty could enjoy a meal together. She claimed it was necessary to keep from having to serve food multiple times, but Savanah knew it was Mrs. B's way of bringing them together as a community. After Mr. B said grace, everyone seemed to enjoy the downtime to share a meal but Savanah picked at her food, unable to get Corey's news off her mind.

She looked down the table to where her fourteen-year-old daughter Kendra sat next to Pete's son, Beau. Savanah sighed heavily.

"Don't worry," Jason said, touching her arm lightly.

"I was fourteen once. Of course, I'll worry." Jason looked perplexed, and Savanah nodded toward Kendra.

His mouth formed an O, and he nodded. "Want me to have a talk with him?"

Savanah thought about it for a moment. "Maybe you should talk to Pete first."

She was pushing her roasted turnips around her plate when she heard Gabby calling for Jason. He stood and pushed his chair back. "What is it?"

Gabby bent and placed her hands on her knees, trying to catch her breath while Savanah wracked her brain, trying to recall which guard post Gabby had been stationed at. Finally catching her breath and straightening, she said, "Valson's back."

FIVE

Savanah

Event + Three Months

Savanah pushed light brown locks of hair from her forehead with the back of her hand, leaving streaks of flour behind. She looked up from the dough she'd been kneading to see Jason and Blake walking toward the house. Jason's face was expressionless. In the two weeks since her brother, Valson's return, he'd been out everyday searching. He hadn't found what he'd been looking for—or whom.

It had been two months since the military came through and disrupted the Blanchard family's control over the community of Vincent, and still there had been no sightings of his mother, sisters, or cousins. They'd found the bodies of his uncles and brothers, so he at least had some resolution. Blake was carrying an extra rifle—a hunting rifle.

Maybe their trip wasn't a total waste.

"Hi," Savanah said as they approached.

The corners of Jason's mouth curled slightly and then fell back into a straight line. He was trying. Savanah knew grief was messy

36

—even if the relationship with the deceased wasn't perfect. At least that's how it had been with the death of her father. Waves of grief still crashed over her at times, even now. She understood Jason's pain.

"Any luck finding ammo?" she asked, pointing to the Winchester rifle Blake held.

"Some—not enough," he replied.

They looked exhausted. Everyone was, but those that ventured out away from the farm and its roadblocks seemed to be hit the worst. They'd witnessed firsthand the death and destruction beyond Sugar Cove Road. The others were somewhat insulated from it—for now, at least.

"We're going to try going farther west in a day or two," Jason said. He took two steps toward her, leaned down, and kissed her on the top of her head.

"Go inside and get a bite to eat and then get some rest. Everything is taken care of for today," Savanah said.

He reached down and cupped her chin in the palm of his right hand, raised it, and studied her face. The intensity of his gaze was too much. She wanted to look away and didn't understand why. It could be that she felt old, dirty, and unattractive. The last two months had not been kind to her body—her mind—her spirit.

"You look tired yourself. You should ask for help more," Jason said.

"Kendra is coming to help me right after she gets back from Mrs. B's."

"How's she doing today?"

"The same," Savanah said, her tone flat.

Mrs. Bertrand had fallen ill two weeks before. It had started with a headache, and then the chills and body aches began the next day. Mr. Bertrand was down a few days, though he was able to bounce back but none of Savanah's herbal remedies seemed to be working for Mrs. B. Her cough was worse, and she was so weak.

Kendra had been taking her over some bone broth and a hibiscus and rosehip tea.

"Maybe Pete and Rob will bring antibiotics back with them," Jason said.

"Hopefully."

"How're your in-laws?" Savanah asked, directing her question to Blake.

Blake's gaze turned toward the ground. "It's not looking good. They both have pretty high fevers. My wife is just beside herself."

"I'm sorry." Savanah said that a lot lately. She was sick of saying and hearing it. Everyone seemed to be sorry. She just wanted this whole nightmare to end, but there was no end in sight.

She forced a smile. "Pete and Rob will bring antibiotics from the army base. They'll be fine in a few days." She knew it was a lie. Blake knew it too. There was no way the military would give up valuable antibiotics or other medications when their soldiers needed them to continue fighting this damn war.

Blake lifted a hand in the air and nodded. "I better get on home," he said weakly.

Savanah watched him walk toward the gate to the pasture. As he lifted the latch, she said, "Thank you, Blake. Thank you for continuing to try."

He stopped and turned. "No need to thank me, Savanah. We're in this together."

That they were. They all needed one another. Just two months earlier, they'd all gone about their separate lives, and now they must depend on one another for security and sustenance.

Jason wrapped his arms around Savanah and held her tight. She melted into him, tears stinging her eyes. She feared that if she let go, they would be like a tsunami overtaking and drowning her. It was just so damn hard to remain positive and hopeful as things continued to get harder every day.

"Come inside with me. Let's both get something to eat and take a nap. You can't keep pushing yourself like this. The kids need you."

That last part was like a knife to the heart. She was doing everything she could think of to keep life as normal as possible for them, but death and misery were all around, and she couldn't always protect them from it.

"When Kendra gets back, I'll come inside and rest a minute." She lied. There was too much to do, and she knew she wouldn't truly rest, anyway. She had laundry and dishes still to do. She needed to go through her books and see if she could find anything more she could do for the Bertrands and Blake's in-laws. The herbal teas and chest salves seemed to have helped the children, and those who had been sick were fully recovered now. She hoped the worst of the flu season was behind them. Was that wishful thinking?

Jason pulled up a chair and sat across from her. "I'll go in when you do then."

She shot him a dirty look and tossed the hand towel she'd been holding onto the table. "Okay. Okay. Let me cover this dough, and I'll go in, and I'll make you some eggs."

Jason smiled. A genuine smile where his teeth showed and that sparkle she loved twinkled in his eyes. "How about I make you pancakes?"

She cocked her head ever so slightly and batted her eyelashes. "You found syrup?"

His head bobbed. "I did."

Savanah closed her eyes and licked her lips. She'd taken her family off refined sugar long before the world collapsed, but they'd always enjoyed honey and fruits. It had been at least six weeks since she'd tasted anything sweet.

"What do you say?" Jason said, his strong chin jutting out. He looked so damn handsome—she was tempted.

"You'll have to make enough for the kids."

She could see Jason deflate somewhat, and then his lips curled up. "Awesome."

Even though she knew he was disappointed that she'd put him off again, Savanah knew Jason understood. She was a good Catholic girl and was raising her children the same way her grandmother had raised her. She wasn't going to set all that aside just because the world had changed. When the time was right, they'd go into town and see the priest. Until then, she'd make sure she and Jason never ate pancakes alone.

The pancakes were amazing, and the kids were ecstatic. Keegan, being the kind little soul that he was, saved some of his to share with his friend, Jeremy; he and his parents had arrived just a few days earlier. Savanah and Jason left Kendra and Karson in charge of the dishes and moved into the living room to discuss what he and Blake had seen on their journey outside the community.

"No sign of your family?" Savanah asked as she lowered herself onto her grandmother's old armchair, running her hand along the arm and feeling her calming presence.

"No."

"Were there many survivors east of town?"

"There aren't many left. The ones who've stayed said most had headed to Shreveport or Texarkana to the shelters there."

"I wonder if anyone's made it there?" Savanah asked, more to herself than Jason.

They had no way of knowing and had all heard rumors of the bandits preying on the refugees along those routes. The tales of the robbing, rape, and murders were just one of the reasons Savanah and the others hadn't considered leaving. Life inside some government-run camp didn't sound much better than what they were experiencing on their own. The only thing the government might offer that was better was some measure of safety.

But as long as they had armed guards, they would be able to continue to provide what little they had to the survivors who'd taken refuge there with them on Sugar Cove Road. Savanah couldn't think about any other scenario. She prayed that whatever came against them, they'd be stronger and faster and that their luck would hold out until the military could defeat the Chinese and put the country back together.

SIX

Isabella

CALCASIEU PARISH, LOUISIANA

Event + Three Months

Isabella stood at the kitchen sink, staring out at the children who were playing a game of tag in the backyard. Children were so resilient. Despite the lack of technology, the shortage of food, and the threats of war and marauders, they continued to laugh and play. Kylie shoved Keegan to the ground, and Kendra ran to pick him up, just as Isabella imagined she'd done multiple times before the event that had changed all their lives.

The adults that had gathered to form a safe community strived to make the children's lives as normal as possible. Isabella could understand why, but she questioned whether it was really the best for them. The world beyond their roadblocks was a dangerous and uncertain place. To survive, wouldn't they all need to be prepared for whatever may come? Could you prepare a six-year-old?

Isabella thought about the little girl they'd nearly run over back in Houston. Her parents had left to find food for her and her little brother and never returned. If Jaz hadn't stubbornly swooped them up and taken them to the church, what would have become of the two small children alone in the big city? Would Savanah's children be prepared to care for themselves if trouble found them here? Kendra and Karson were very much more capable than most adults Isabella knew, but could they keep themselves and their siblings alive in this new world?

"They seem so carefree, don't they?" Savanah said as she walked up behind Isabella and placed her hand on the counter to steady herself.

"Are you all right?" Isabella asked.

Savanah looked up. She did not look all right. Her face was pale.

Savanah wiped the sweat from her brow and lowered her head. "I just felt a little lightheaded. It's probably dehydration. I haven't been drinking enough water lately."

Or eating enough, Isabella thought. The food rationing was starting to take its toll on everyone, but Savanah was hiding the fact that she was giving most of her meals to her children. What Savanah didn't know was that her daughter Kendra was doing the same thing. She'd overheard Kendra scolding Kylie for wasting her food on her kitten when she had gone without for her to have it.

"Why don't you sit for a while and rest?" Isabella suggested, taking Savanah's arm, and leading her to a kitchen chair. "I'll get you a glass of water."

Isabella placed the glass in front of Savanah and lowered herself onto the seat beside her. She placed a hand on Savanah's. "You have to take care of yourself too. You have to eat more. You can't let yourself get run down. Your children need you healthy."

Savanah looked at her with such contempt that Isabella was taken aback. She withdrew her hand, knowing that she'd overstepped her bounds. "I'm sorry. I'm not a mother. I can't imagine…"

"No! No, you cannot imagine," Savanah snapped.

Isabella choked back tears. She wanted to excuse herself and escape what she suspected would come next, but she stayed put. No matter how uncomfortable it was, Savanah needed to be able to release her pain and fears to someone, and Isabella wanted to be there for her.

Savanah lowered her gaze. A single tear slid down her cheek, and she wiped it away with the back of her hand, staring toward the window and the sound of her children, who were now back to squealing with laughter. "I'm sorry."

"No need to apologize, Savanah."

"It's so damn hard. This is not the world I wanted for them. I fear for them every minute. I can't sleep for worrying what horrible thing could rain down on us at any moment." The tears were flowing in a steady stream now and Savanah wiped her nose with the hem of her shirt. "I've taken care of them every day of their lives—me. I did it all by myself because I couldn't rely on their good-for-nothing father." She looked up at the ceiling and ran a hand down the length of her braided hair. "If my grandparents hadn't left us this place, I don't know what I would have done. It has sustained us. But I fear that it won't be enough—nothing I do will be enough."

"You are no longer alone, Savanah. Will is here. Look out that window. Look at all those people your homestead is sheltering and sustaining. They are here for you too. We're all in this together. You have to let us help you now."

Savanah turned her gaze to Isabella, and they stared at one another for a moment as Isabella's words sank in. Savanah shot from her chair and grabbed Isabella, pulling her into a firm embrace. "Thank you! Thank you so very much. You're right. You're so right. We can do this—together. We can. We are no longer alone."

Isabella rocked her gently and allowed her to relax into that truth before stepping away and guiding Savanah back to her chair. "You sit here. I'm going to make you a bowl of soup. And you are going to eat it all." Isabella turned toward the tiny wood stove where the day's main meal was simmering. As she ladled a scoop into a bowl, Isabella inhaled deeply, attempting to rein in her own emotions and head off a torrent of tears. She had her own fears about what their future held. As she and Will grew closer, her fear of losing him and Cayden increased. She pushed the thoughts away and placed a spoon inside the bowl before setting it in front of Savanah.

"You don't have to worry about your children going hungry. Will would never let that happen—ever. We will find a way. The groups that went out yesterday will bring back something."

Savanah picked up the spoon and blew on the steaming broth. "I know. Will is doing everything he can. He's running himself ragged. He won't stop or slow down until we are all safe and cared for. That's my brother." She tasted the soup and placed the spoon back into the bowl.

"They'll find game, canned goods, or something today. It will be all right." Isabella turned to put the lid back onto the soup pot. They had enough for everyone to eat today and maybe tomorrow. Someone would find something for the day after that, but eventually, there'd be nothing left to find. They'd be forced to move north in search of food, even if the war stayed away from them. Would it be too late? Would they be fit enough for the journey? Isabella feared not all of them would be.

"I was thinking we should butcher the remaining hog," Savanah said, standing and placing her empty bowl into the dishpan sitting on the counter. She stared out the window. "That should get us by a few more days."

Isabella knew how hard the decision had been for her to make. The sow was one of the last of her animals left. They'd eaten the goats and most of the chickens in the first few weeks. They'd butchered the boar and another sow two weeks ago, and at the time, it had seemed like so much food, but with so many mouths to feed, it hadn't lasted long. They were using the last of the smoked jowls and hocks in the soups, were extremely low on beans, and the rice was all but gone. They had maybe a day or two before they had nothing at all, so it wasn't a choice of whether to butcher the hog or not. It was just a matter of when.

"I'll have the guys fetch the water for the hog bath," Isabella said. She'd received a crash course in processing farm animals in the time she'd been on the homestead. Everyone pitched in. Isabella couldn't imagine Savanah doing the task on her own and assumed that she'd taken them to a meat processor before the lights went out.

Savanah turned toward the back door. "I'll have Karson and Keegan bring more firewood over to the outdoor kitchen and get the smoker ready."

Isabella smiled. "I'm looking forward to pork rinds again."

Savanah placed her hand on the doorknob and looked back. The corners of her mouth turned up in a forced smile, but her eyes displayed her true emotions. "Me too. I know Karson and Keegan will be thrilled. They love cracklings."

They wouldn't have time to cure the pork belly for bacon. That would take days just for the salt to pull the liquid out of the meat. They'd likely just roast the whole hog and feed everyone. Anything left would be put in the smoker.

"I'll take some soup over to Mr. and Mrs. B and then come help process it with you," Isabella said.

"Here." Savanah reached for a jar on the counter. "I found echinacea and goldenseal to help with the congestion."

Isabella took the jar from her and stuffed it into the backpack with the thermos of soup. "They'll get better," she said, forcing a smile. The last time she'd seen Mrs. B, she'd wondered if the elderly woman would make it through the night and been surprised when Kendra had sent word back that she was awake. Isabella pulled the neck gaiter down over her head in preparation for covering her mouth and nose when she reached the Bertrands' home. The last thing she wanted was to come down with the flu as well. There were too many sick people to take care of as it was, and Will didn't need any more to worry about.

Savanah pointed to the neck gaiter face mask. "Wear the surgical mask underneath it. We'll have the search team look for more to replace it. We should take all the precautions we can."

Isabella nodded and pulled a mask from the box on the shelf above the sink. The number of things they'd taken for granted before the lights went out struck her. Before, she'd hardly thought anything of entering a home where someone had the flu. She'd just keep her distance and remember to wash her hands. If she still managed to get sick, her doctor would prescribe something, and it would resolve without complication in a few days. Not anymore. All their bodies were worn down and immunity so fragile that something like that could take even the strongest person out.

SEVEN

Will
___

Event + Three Months

Will barely touched his soup at the group's midday meal. A knot formed in the pit of his stomach as everyone was finishing up. He stood and cleared his throat. "Everyone, I have something that I'd like to discuss."

Heads bobbed as Will described the scarcity of food, the ever-present danger from the marauders roaming the countryside in search of the same resources as they needed, and the looming reality of the war being waged along the Louisiana coastline. As he spoke, Will paid particular attention to Savanah's body language. She was the main person he was interested in persuading.

"We're all well aware of the challenges we currently face, Will. What's your point?" Savanah asked, standing with her bowl in her hand. She was a very intelligent woman. She knew where Will was going with this.

"I've been giving it a lot of thought." Will glanced over at Walker and then at Isabella. He'd spoken to Isabella only briefly about going north. She looked from Will to Savanah. He probably should have told her he was bringing the issue to the community. "I think we should be prepared to head north."

Savanah's eyes narrowed, and her lips twitched. She held his gaze.

"I think we should have a backup plan ready to execute should things force us to bug out."

"Bug out?" Savanah asked, her pitching high.

"Yes. Like when we prepare to evacuate in advance of a hurricane," Will said.

Jane, who was seated two chairs down from Savanah was nodding. "Luca and I have our go-bags packed and ready."

Pete Ashby's wife spoke up. "I agree. We're all well versed in the need to be ready to evacuate. Usually, we have a few days' notice as the Hurricane Center figures out where the storm will make landfall, but in this instance, we're not likely to have much warning. My family is ready. We've been discussing and practicing bugging out. Everyone knows what to do and where to meet up if we're separated."

Savanah cocked her head to the side and stared at her. Will was happy to hear that others shared his thoughts on the matter. It wasn't just him being paranoid. That would go a long way with Savanah. Besides, if the Ashbys and Jane and Luca left, it would put quite a strain on the group. It would mean longer hours on guard duty and less time for searching for food and taking care of things around the homestead.

"I get that everyone is well versed in evacuation planning, and we all should be prepared, but there is still much we could do to secure this place and to—"

Jason stood and placed a hand on Savanah's shoulder. "Will's right. We need to have this discussion. We've needed to talk this through, and I'm glad you brought it up today, Will."

Savanah looked like she'd been slapped. Will was sure she felt blindsided. That hadn't been his intention. Jason's hand gently slid down Savanah's arm. He took her hand in his and held it up to his chest. "I know you feel that staying here on your grandparents' homestead is the safest and best option for the long term, but we must consider a backup plan." Jason turned to Will. "Were you thinking of heading toward Shreveport?"

Will was so taken aback by Jason Blanchard that he stammered as he responded. "I, um… I was thinking of going farther north and pushing on to Texarkana actually. They have a shelter there that can sustain us until we can find a more permanent solution. I was considering using it as a base to push into Arkansas in search of somewhere with more natural resources and fewer people."

Jason put his arm around Savanah's shoulder. She looked up at him with tears in her eyes and it pained Will's heart to see her so troubled by the prospect.

"Migration has been used by refugees for survival for thousands of years. It would be difficult, I'm sure, but it might be our best option," Jason said.

Will was relieved that Jason was on his side in the matter. He'd misjudged the man. It was clear now that he truly cared for Savanah and the kids. If she wouldn't listen to Will, maybe she'd listen to Jason.

Savanah's head dropped, and her shoulders slumped. She wiped a tear from her cheek and then nodded. "Okay. Okay. We can discuss a plan and prepare ourselves in case it comes to that…"

"Savanah," Jason turned her toward him and took her face in the palms of his hands. "Sweetheart. It *has* come to that. If we don't leave now, we won't have the ability or strength to go later. We can't wait until we are all sick and malnourished to go. We have to be smart here. Look at you. You've lost at least twenty pounds since the lights went out, and you were thin to start with. You can't keep giving all your food to the children and expect to walk two hundred and fifty miles to Texarkana. You wouldn't make it ten miles before I'd be carrying you."

"I'm sorry," Savanah said. She turned back toward Will. "It's just all the stories I've heard about your journey here and about how the refugees are being attacked as they head north. I'm scared as hell..." She swallowed hard before continuing. "For the children."

Walker stood and made his way around the table to stand next to Will. "I can assure you that I, for one, will do everything within my power to protect those kids. We've been scouting alternative routes, ones not so traveled and hopefully not so attractive to the raiders. I feel confident that we can make it to Texarkana safely."

Savanah wiped tears from her eyes with the back of her hand. "I appreciate that, Walker. I know you're all correct. We need to do something. I just hate to give up on this place." Her eyes scanned the house and the now nearly empty barn.

Will stepped toward his sister and touched her shoulder. "Maybe it's not forever. When things get back to normal, we'll come back, and I'll help you rebuild."

She smiled, and then her head bobbed slightly. "Maybe."

"We'll make it. Together we'll all make it," Will said, hoping he sounded convincing. In all honesty, he knew the odds of that were slim, but they had to try. What choice did they have?

"I'll finish getting the kids' go-bags ready," Savanah said, wiping another tear from the corner of her eye.

Isabella pushed herself away from the table. Will's heart nearly skipped a beat as she flipped her burnt umber-colored hair over her shoulder. "I'll help you, Savanah. I'll help Kylie pick her favorite toy." A smile tugged at the corners of Will's lips. He felt so very blessed to have her in his life—especially in these brutal days. Her kindness and giving nature was like a salve to his wounded soul— not just his, but Cayden's as well. And now she extended her generous nature toward his sister and her kids. She glanced his way and nodded slightly—her way of reassuring him that everything was going to be all right. Somehow, he felt that it would. She gave him hope, not just that they'd all make it safely to Texarkana, but that they'd find a way not just to survive but truly live.

"I'm going to check on Mr. and Mrs. Bertrand. I found some

books that Mrs. B might like," Jane said, picking up a stack of paperbacks. She walked closer and leaned in. "You know there's no way they'd make it even a mile, right?"

Will drew in a deep breath and let it out. He'd tried very hard not to think about them and at that moment, he resented Jane for bringing it up and spoiling his positive mood. His head bobbed twice, and then he turned away from her. What could he say? They couldn't wait for the older couple to recover and grow stronger— that wasn't likely to happen—not without modern medicine and proper nutrition. Mr. B was refusing meals and giving them to his wife. He'd been a slight man before the lights went out. Now he looked frail and gaunt.

No, they wouldn't make it a mile. They wouldn't make it to their front gate. As Will's face contorted with the anguish of the thought, he felt a firm hand on his shoulder.

"We can make a cart and pull them," Walker said as he stepped in front of Will.

Their eyes met, and then Will looked away. "They'd never allow that."

"Mr. B would. He'd do anything to save his wife. I am in awe of the love between them after all these years together. It's a rare and powerful thing. Don't underestimate it."

"He wouldn't put the kids at risk. He's a very astute and proud man. He knows they'd slow us down which would put everyone in danger." Will sighed. "He's the real deal—he and Mrs. B. They've lived a true Christian life. They're selfless."

"Maybe I could—"

"You can try," Will said, interrupting him. "Unless you can guarantee they wouldn't put the others in danger, you will fail."

Walker lifted his chin, and his shoulders moved back. "We'll just have to find a way for them not to slow us down then. Leaving them behind to die alone is not an option."

A pang of guilt stabbed at Will's heart. Of course, Walker was right. He admired him for his fortitude and empathy. It was just that Will was so fatigued and suffering from brain fog that he couldn't think of a way to do that.

"I'll work on it," Walker said. "I'll come up with something. When I do, I'll inform the Bertrands and help them get ready to leave."

Will just bobbed his head and prayed that Walker's mission succeeded. How would he explain leaving them behind to his son? He'd grown so close to them since they'd arrived and considered them as grandparents. There was no way his tenderhearted boy would understand that it was for the good of the community.

He looked around as the others picked up their dishes and went back to their chores. Traveling with such a large group would have its challenges, especially with several elderly and so many children, but Will felt they were better prepared than most of the folks heading out on the road. With the information that Jane, Luca, and the others would soon bring back, they could send out scouts and secure checkpoints ahead of the group's arrival. They would make this trip as safe as possible. They'd learned a few things from observing the military movements. Will hoped it would be enough. It had to be.

EIGHT

Will

Over the next few days, following the community's discussion regarding finalizing preparations to leave and head north, Will had spent less time at the roadblocks and looking for Jason's kin, and instead gone out with the scouting teams to reassure himself of the soundness of their proposed route.

The plan was to stay off the main highways that were used by most refugees and had become the prime feeding grounds for the bandits and evildoers seeking to prey on the innocent and helpless. Instead, the group would travel the back roads, only crossing major highways under the cover of darkness when they were less likely to be spotted. Two teams of scouts would go in advance of the group, hopefully, to steer them away from any trouble spots.

They'd picked several places in which to camp. Abandoned farms with large barns, a grove of cypress trees near a canal just south of Perkins. A warehouse in Roseville. They'd even pre-positioned some supplies along their preferred route and one alternate in case they needed to sit tight for a day or two or if they were attacked and lost supplies. Pete Ashby had been thorough in his planning and Will admired the man's survival skills. It was as if he'd been preparing for something like this disaster all along—maybe he had. He had seemed well supplied for it at least.

After hearing the plan and seeing the route—at least the beginning section, Will felt better about their chances of actually getting the majority of their forty-plus person troop safely to Texarkana. He was still very much concerned about what they would find there. The idea of entering an overcrowded government-run camp was not ideal. They'd be disarmed. He was certain of that. They'd be separated for sure. They might be able to keep families together, but not all the families and not everyone together in one shelter. It would make coordinating their planned scouting missions outside of the FEMA run camp more difficult. Would they even allow them to leave? Once they did, could they return to their families? There were just too many unknowns for Will to feel okay with that part of his plan.

Finding somewhere for the group to go after the shelter was imperative to their long-term survival though. It absolutely had to happen, so they'd have to make it work somehow, even if the whole group had to leave the safety of the shelter to push farther north into the wilds of Arkansas. Will was certain that life at the shelter would be unsustainable, if not physically—mentally.

The two-man team ahead stopped. One of Pete's brothers turned and flashed hand signals which led Pete to signal the rest of the six men and women following him on this scouting mission to stop in their tracks. Luca ran up to Pete's position. The two men spoke in hushed voices before Luca ran back to the group. "Team Alpha spotted movement on the road. Six men, two women. All heavily armed and carrying large packs. It could be marauders or well-stocked travelers. In any case, Pete wants to let them pass before pushing on."

Jane nodded. "Copy that."

Will glanced over at her. This wasn't Jane and Luca's first scouting mission with Pete and his team which mostly comprised his family members and close friends. It appeared that

Jane had picked up on their lingo and Luca seemed to understand the hand signals. They were motivated. Will could understand why. They had a child to think about. The baby growing inside Jane propelled them to find a route to Texarkana that would present the least risk to the unborn child and lead them to the safety of a camp with a doctor and supplies for a baby.

Will wanted to see his family out of harm's way as well. He wouldn't rest until he had but he was a pragmatist. He knew the road ahead would not be easy—not by a long shot—no matter how much they planned.

Jane relocated to a well-shaded spot beneath a tree and leaned against its trunk, pulled out a protein bar, just one of the supplies Pete had shared with the team before they headed out, and unwrapped it. She ate while they waited. Will was saving his bar for when he really needed a pick-me-up. So far, pure adrenaline had sustained him.

Within fifteen minutes, the group on the road had passed and the advance team had signaled for them to continue forward. They crossed the highway and into a gully before reaching an open field. Will searched the faces of those who'd traveled this section of the route before, looking for any sign of concern. They seemed relaxed. Pete and his son Beau were ever vigilant as usual, with their rifles scanning the woodline and the way ahead. Will pulled his rifle closer to his chest as they walked through knee-high grass. It wasn't just people that concerned him. Who knew what kind of threat crawled the ground concealed in the weeds? It would so suck to get bitten by a snake. He just hoped that the bug spray Isabella had found would ward off ticks and chiggers. Those two tiny creatures could also cause a world of hurt and carry debili-tating disease within their saliva.

As they neared a high, weathered barn at the edge of the field, Pete halted them by a fist in the air as he had done previously. The others in the rear stopped and dropped to one knee in the grass. Will reluctantly followed suit. He watched as the lead team approached the barn and entered through a side door. A minute later, one of the men ran back to have a conversation with Pete. Something was wrong. Will could sense it. Pete made hand motions, waving the rest of them back toward the trees. Jane sucked in a deep breath.

"What is it?" Will whispered.

"Squatters most likely," Luca replied.

"What does that mean for the mission?" Will asked as they hurriedly moved toward the woodline and concealment.

"They could just be staying the night like we plan to do, or they could have set up camp. We won't know until the team assesses the situation."

"How would they know?"

"They'll likely ask them."

"Politely," Jane said.

Politely? She'd said it like there was some other way to do it. Maybe they'd not done so very nicely in the past. She'd pointed it out for a reason. It was something he'd make a note of asking her about later. He needed to know as much about this team as possible if he were going to trust them to lead his family out on the road.

NINE

Walker

CALCASIEU PARISH, LOUISIANA

Event + Three Months

Just one day after Will had returned from the scouting mission, all hell broke loose and the time had arrived for them to put the plan into action. They had no choice. It was now—or never.

Walker was oiling the springs on an old pony cart he'd found in a barn about three miles from the homestead. He'd searched every barn for miles and it was the best he could find. It was rusty, and the footboards rotted out, but he'd been working on it as he looked for an animal capable of pulling it. He had been just about to lose hope of finding anything that had not become someone's last meal when he'd come upon a pony feeding on bramble leaves in the woods as he crossed from one farm to the next. He was a cunning little fellow, hiding out like that and it had taken the better part of a day to get near enough to get a halter on him. The children had been thrilled to see him and all clamored around asking for pony rides, but this was for the Bertrands, and he needed him in tip-top shape for their journey. So, as hard as it was to see all the disappointed faces, he'd said no to rides. Kylie and Keegan had been content to help him bathe and brush the little guy.

Walker squirted more oil on the springs and then bounced up and down, testing them. He wanted as smooth a ride as he could give Mrs. B, knowing that would be important to Mr. Bertrand. He was incredibly touched by the love the two shared even after all these years in this deep hardship and the trials they all were facing.

When he heard footfalls on the gravel drive, Walker hopped down from the buggy and ran to the open barn door. He stopped in his tracks when he heard the kid, through gasped breaths, spout out, "A runner from Choupique is at the checkpoint down on Highway 108." Beau was huffing so bad that Walker could barely make out what he was saying, but it must be bad for the kid to have run all that way, and he had run hard by the looks of him. He was drenched in sweat, scraped and cut from apparent falls, and dirty from head to toe from fording canals and gullies. Whatever it was —it was bad news.

Will met the kid in the middle of the drive and placed a hand on the boy's shoulder. "Just take a deep breath. Inhale slowly. Now exhale, slowly, Beau."

Beau did as he was instructed, and when he could speak, Will asked him, "Have the Chinese broken through the American lines?"

The boy nodded. His eyes were wide. His jaw clenched tight.

"How close?"

"Ten miles and moving fast. They're in a hurry," the kid said through gritted teeth. He rubbed his scraped palms on his filthy jeans.

"Let's get you inside and have someone clean up those cuts while I round everyone up."

"Are we leaving now?" the boy asked, almost in a whisper.

"Yes. We have no choice."

"The Bertrands?"

Will sucked in a breath. It was too painful to acknowledge to himself, let alone to this boy.

"Walker will try."

Walker's heart leaped. It was the moment he'd been dreading.

"He won't go."

"I know. But Walker is pretty persuasive. There's a chance. Now, there's no time to waste. Get cleaned up and get into position."

Walker choked up upon hearing the confidence Will placed in him. It only increased the pressure to succeed.

"Yes, sir."

Will glanced back over his shoulder at the kid as he ran toward the gate, likely to alert Pete and his team. They'd need to know first and head out in front of the group. The time of preparations had ended, and it was now time to put them to the test. Walker prayed they passed muster.

Walker took off to catch up to Will. He needed to know where his mind was at—what he was thinking.

"Did you hear?" Will asked as Walker approached him as he opened the gate.

"Yes. I'm heading to the Bertrands. Unless you need me somewhere else."

"No. Not right now. You go and try to convince that old codger to come with us. After that, will you help Victory round up all five of her children? That youngest is always running off, and we don't have time for a game of hide and seek right now."

"I'll round them up and get them to the barn. I'll make sure no one is left behind, Will."

Will's lips formed a slight smile. "I know you will try your best, Walker. That is all we can do." We're so lucky to have you. Your knowledge and fortitude are so needed—more than you could ever know."

"Thanks, Will. Anything I can do to help—I'm there."

"I know." Will stepped through the gate, stopped, and turned to face Walker. "That is what I admire about you most, I think."

Walker looked away.

"You're selfless, Walker. These people are practically strangers to you, but here you are."

"It's my duty," Walker mumbled.

"Before you go to the Bertrands, will you find Isabella and tell her where I've gone and why?"

Walker nodded. He knew that it really should come from Will, but he understood the urgency of the moment. There just wasn't time. They'd run out of time. He'd run out of time. His task was at hand. He couldn't afford to fail. He couldn't live with that on his conscience. The Bertrands deserved a chance as much as anyone else. He wanted to give that to the elderly couple. He felt compelled yet didn't know why. Maybe it was the memories of his grandfather and the helplessness he'd seen on his face as he watched Walker's grandmother wither away under Alzheimer's. Mr. B reminded him of his grandfather, but it was more than that. It went against his humanity to consider abandoning the old couple to what would come if they were left behind.

Savanah was in the kitchen when Walker burst through the door. She drew in a breath and held it.

"It's time," Walker said.

"Where's Will? Jason?" Savanah asked in a near whisper.

"Will ran to get Pete and his boys. He wanted me to inform everyone here. Where's Isabella and Cayden?"

"Isabella?" Savanah asked, looking toward the door. She looked confused. They were likely spread over the two homesteads with Kendra tending to the Bertrands, and Kylie off God knows where. It was hard keeping track of them with so many places for them to be.

Savanah returned her gaze to Walker. "I don't know where she is."

"That's okay. I'll find her before I head over to the Bertrands. Do you need me to help you with the kids?"

"My kids," she whispered. Her hand flew up to her neck.

Walker was a trained observer. His law enforcement experience had alerted him to her panicked state. He walked over, placed a hand on her now trembling shoulder, and spoke softly. "It's going to be all right. We've practiced this over and over. Everyone knows what to do. I will sound the alarm, and everyone will come running —even Kylie. She knows there's a treat waiting for her if she does."

That had been his idea. He and Kylie had an understanding.

"Thank you, Walker. I'll sound the alarm. You go do what you need to do. I pray you succeed; Mr. B is a stubborn old cuss."

He straightened and removed his hand from hers. "You sure?"

"I'm sure. You're right. When everyone hears the alarm, they'll all come running. I'll have more help than I know what to do with."

"Okay. I'll be back in a jiffy with the Bertrands. We're going to make it in time, Savanah. Have faith."

Faith was something in short supply these days. It seemed that every day only brought more sorrow with no possible end in sight.

"Thanks," she said.

Walker found Isabella in one of the RVs helping care for a sick child. She took a deep breath as Walker explained the news the kid had brought and where Will had run off to. She stiffened her spine and gathered herself with grace but took it seemingly in stride. Walker watched her go through the process of acceptance and move into action. She gave him a curt nod. "All right. It's go-time. We all have lots to do, Walker. Godspeed with the Bertrands."

"Thanks, Isabella. I may well need God's intervention on this one."

~

Walker wasted no time rushing back to the barn to hook the pony to the cart. He threw the blankets into the back of the short wagon and yanked on the pony's reins. He jerked his head a few times, but Walker was firm and insistent. The animal yielded to the tug and moved through the barn door, down the drive, and out onto the pavement. As Walker pulled the pony and cart toward the Bertrands' house, he saw their front door open, and Mr. B stepped out onto the porch, shutting the door behind him.

"Walker," Mr. Bertrand said, stuffing his hands into the front pockets of his blue Dickies work pants.

"We received news from down south. It's time," Walker blurted out. It wasn't how the conversation had gone in his head. He'd rehearsed a different approach, but he could tell from Mr. B's tone that the soft approach wasn't going to work.

"And the cart?"

"For Mrs. B."

"Come on inside."

The smell of Savanah's herbs brewing on the stove filled the house. Mr. B led Walker to the master bedroom, where Mrs. Bertrand lay covered to her chin with blankets. The sight of her wrenched Walker's heart; she looked so frail. Her hair had been lovingly combed and a braid pulled to one side. Her eyes opened as they entered the room. She turned toward the door, and Walker could see her struggle to focus.

"Good afternoon, Mrs. B, I'm sorry—"

"Don't be. I love to have visitors, especially handsome ones like yourself." Her lips curled up and then fell. "But from the sound of those hooves on my drive, I imagine this is something more than a social call."

"I came to fetch you. It's time. The Chinese have broken through, and they're advancing quickly."

She turned her head ever so slightly toward her husband. They stared at one another for a long moment before she spoke. "We appreciate your concern, Walker, and all the trouble you've gone to on our—my—behalf, but we're still firm in our stance. Her eyes scanned the dresser to her right where framed photos had been lovingly placed of her children, grandchildren, and likely even great-grandchildren.

"This here is our home and has been so for over sixty years. I've lived a long and wonderfully blessed life. I want to stay here in my own bed for whatever time I have left—even if it is only hours or days." She turned, and their eyes met. "You might not understand that, Walker, but I pray that you live long enough that you see your golden days, and then you will."

"Mrs. B. This doesn't have to be—"

"It's my decision. I've made up my mind, and I'm not going."

Walker's gaze fell to Mr. B, who now stood at the foot of the bed looking down upon his wife. Walker was immediately taken back to the scene of his grandfather, but he didn't see that same helpless and hopeless look. They had resigned themselves to their fate. They seemed so calm in the face of it all. How could they be? How did one lose that innate sense of self-preservation?

"You're a leader, Walker. They need you. Will and Jason have families to protect and look out for. You, you can see the bigger picture and take care of the whole group. Pete and his boys will be concerned with completing the mission with success but ultimately, they too will make their families their top priority. The community needs you as the leader to look out for everyone's well-being. You're up to the task. Don't doubt yourself. God will go before you. He will strengthen and guide you. You'll know the right things to do. You'll be instrumental in getting everyone there safely. It may mean making tough calls and being stern when the others need it. You're up to that as well. Your training will carry you through, I'm sure. You are the man for this job, Walker. You won't fail. And God won't fail you."

A lump had formed in Walker's throat. It meant so much coming from a man like Mr. Bertrand. Having his vote of confidence was uplifting, even though Walker didn't see himself in that light. He'd do whatever it took—that was the truth—but the leadership role would remain with Will, Jason, and Pete. And he was fine with that.

"They need you too, Mr. B. They need your guidance and godly wisdom. It's the one absolutely necessary thing that the community lacks."

"I appreciate that, son. But we've made up our minds." Mr. Bertrand lowered himself into the club chair beside his wife's bed, picked up the shotgun, and placed it in his lap. "We're going to stay right here."

TEN

Savanah

Savanah rushed to the outdoor kitchen and pulled on the rough rope tied to the dinner bell. It clanged, and she pulled twice more, waited, and pulled three more times—the signal for trouble.

Karson reached her first. "It's time?"

"Yes, son. You know what to do?"

"Yes, ma'am. I'll get my pack and the little ones' and meet you here."

"And your rifle?"

"Yes, ma'am. I wouldn't forget it. We'll find ammo for it on the way, I bet. I'll make grandpa proud and bag me a big ole buck. You'll see."

She reached out and wrapped her arms around him. "I'm so proud of you, Karson. Do you know that?"

"I'm proud of you. Gran and Granddad would say so too," Karson said as he stepped back.

Savanah's eyes scanned the home her grandfather had built, along with the barn. It was hard to see the pasture and large garden plots with all the campers and tents blocking the view and it hurt her to the core to abandon the place that her family had put so much blood, sweat, and tears into.

"We'll come back," Karson said.

"I know. As soon as this is all over, we'll come back and make it even better than it was," Savanah said, wiping a tear from her cheek.

She caught a glimpse of Jason and some of the others running from the western pasture. "Get your bag, Savanah. I'll get everyone lined up," Jason called as he ran.

"Have you seen Keegan or Kylie?" she asked.

"No. They'll come. Get your pack."

She heard the fear in his voice. It threw her for a moment. He was supposed to be her rock. She couldn't do this. She wasn't ready for this. Not for the road. This could not be happening.

"Go, Savanah!"

She looked back at him as she sprinted toward the house. Their go-bags were lined up by the door. Karson already had his strapped on and was gathering up Kylie's and Keegan's. They met in the doorway. "Do you need me to help you tighten the straps on yours?" he asked.

"No. Take care of your siblings. Make sure theirs are tight. Don't let Kylie fidget and get it too loose."

"I won't."

Savanah mussed his hair as he passed through the door on his way to the meeting spot in front of the house. As she stepped inside, she caught a glimpse of people gathering there through the lace curtains on the front window. She scooped up her pack and plunged her arms through the straps, jumped a few times while pulling down tight on them to make sure they were secure, and turned back toward the door. She stopped, spun around for one last look, and spotted the framed photos lined up on a side table by the far wall. All those baby pictures, vacation photos, and photographs of her parents and grandparents. How could she just leave them behind? How could she leave all this—behind?

"Savanah!" Jason called through the front window. "Let's go!"

She ran to the front door and flung it open expecting to see all four of her children standing in the line next to Jason. All she saw were Karson and Keegan.

"Where's Kylie?" Panic laced her voice. She reached into her pocket and found the piece of butterscotch candy that Walker had promised Kylie. It should have worked. No kid had a sweet tooth like her daughter.

"Kendra is looking for her at the Bertrands. She thought she might have seen Walker heading that way."

Savanah's feet could not move fast enough. She pumped her arms harder and took bigger strides, but her energy level was low. She felt like she was moving in slow motion. Her heart drummed in her ears, drowning out the calls from Jason and Karson to wait. She just kept running.

"Dammit, Kylie. Come out from under there. You cannot take those dump kittens. You know you can't carry them. Let's go," Kendra was saying as Savanah ran toward them. She was yelling. Loudly. She was scared. She was also mad as hell. Kendra was normally a kind and patient child. It took a lot to get her mad, but when she did, she'd let you have it.

"Kylie. Stop being a little brat and get out from under that shed. You heard the bell. We have to go. You're going to get us all killed."

"Go away! I'm not going," Kylie yelled.

Savanah stopped about one hundred feet from the Bertrands' shed. She was drained and out of breath. She bent at the waist and gulped some air, feeling lightheaded. This was not good. Suddenly, things got dark. Savanah fought to stay upright and not pass out.

"Get the hell out here now, Kylie. Do not make me crawl under that filthy, bug-infested shed to get you. If I do, you are going to be so damn sorry."

"You're cussing me. I'm telling Mom."

"I don't freaking care what you tell her. You better get your freaking little butt headed to the house so we can get the freaking hell out of here before the Chinese soldiers kill us all."

"Kendra!" Savanah tried to yell. It came out as a mere squeak. She didn't want her frightening Kylie any more than she already was.

"I want my daddy!" Kylie cried. "I'm waiting here for Daddy. I'm not leaving."

Savanah straightened. Her head swam and vision blurred, yet she pushed on, one step at a time, more feeling her way across the rough sod than seeing. Derek wasn't coming. He'd been killed after Will had been captured and the military rolled through Vincent. She hadn't yet told Kylie that. There just never seemed to be the right time. Now, it appeared they all run out of time. She needed to get to her girls. Things were getting out of control. Kylie could slip out the back and run off into the woods behind the Bertrands' house. It could take hours to find her.

"Kendra! Stop!"

"Let me go!" Kylie screamed at the top of her lungs.

Kendra had hold of her. Savanah prayed she had a tight grip. Kylie was so strong for her age, and if she were fighting to get away, most of the time, she could.

"You're not doing this to Mom. You hear me, brat. You are not going to stress her out like this and hurt her feelings on the day she has to leave our home. She has enough to... Ouch! You bit me!"

"Oh no!" Savanah said. "God, no!"

ELEVEN

Will

When he'd arrived at the rally point on the front lawn of the homestead, Karson had told him about Kylie. He'd run straight for the Bertrands, passing Isabella and Cayden exiting one of the campers, both with their arms full of small children.

"I have to help Savanah find Kylie. I'll meet you," he said, pointing back over his shoulder.

Isabella's eyes grew wide.

"They won't leave without us," he called over his shoulder.

He found Savanah seated on the ground fifty feet from the Bertrands' shed. Kendra was standing next to the door with one of Kylie's shoes in her hand and a stunned look on her face. She stared down at her mother with her mouth open wide.

"Which way?" Will yelled.

Kendra looked up but didn't seem to register the question.

"Kendra! Which way did Kylie run?"

Savanah turned her head in his direction.

"Will," she whimpered.

"Are you all right? Are you hurt?" He stopped briefly by her side.

"No. And no. I'm lightheaded. I'm not hurt," she said. "Will, find my baby."

"I'll get her," he assured her. "Kendra, help your mom back to the house. I'll get Kylie and meet everyone there."

Will didn't wait for a reply. He rounded the shed and took off as fast as he could run toward the canal. That's where she'd have headed. He'd seen her playing there earlier in the day. She had to be there.

~

The weakness in his legs concerned him. He was using a lot of energy. The energy he needed for the road march on which they were all about to embark. They would need to move quickly in order to outpace the advancing enemy army.

He spotted the clearing where he'd seen Kylie earlier and pushed himself harder. His breaths came in gasps as he took them with his mouth wide open, trying to draw as much oxygen into his lungs as possible. He spotted movement through the undergrowth, and his heart lifted. And then...

Kylie's scream pierced his heart like a dagger. He saw her being lifted into the air but couldn't make out by whom. He wanted with all his heart to believe it was someone from their group, but everyone was already gathered on the lawn, ready to go —everyone but Walker and the Bertrands. For a moment, he relaxed, convinced it was Walker. But Kylie would not have screamed like that—not with Walker. They were buddies.

It was the muffled cries that convinced Will that Kylie was indeed in trouble. She was still struggling and fighting to free herself from the man's grasp as Will broke through the brush. The dark-haired man dressed in blue uniform fatigues, narrowed his eyes at Will as he clenched her tighter to his chest, a knife pressed against her tiny throat.

"No!" Will screamed. He held out his hands, palms out,

showing he had no weapons. "No. Don't hurt her. You don't have to do that. I'm not armed. You can just put her down and let her run away. Nothing is going to happen here. Nothing has to happen." Will pleaded with the man but could tell by his hard stare that he wasn't going to give her up easily. Will racked his brain. He had a knife. It was in his front pocket. There was no way he could pull it out, open it, and attack the man before he sliced his niece's throat with his own, very large tactical knife. Will's eyes focused on the man's blade. A trickle of blood seeped out underneath it.

"Please. I beg you. She's just a little girl."

His black eyes were cold and hard. Will took a quick glance around to see if the soldier was alone. Maybe he was. Maybe he'd gotten separated from his unit and he was just scared. Will thought he could work with that scenario. He could promise him safe passage in exchange for Kylie.

"Are you alone? Do you need help? We can help you. I have a vehicle up at the house. You could take it and get to where you need to go." Will lied through his teeth. He hoped—he prayed—the man somehow believed him.

The soldier shifted and looked towards the Bertrands' house.

Yes!

"It's in the barn. It's old. It will run. It has plenty of fuel in it too." Will stepped back, pointing in that direction. "Come on. I'll take you to it."

The man took a step forward, bent slightly to get a better look through the low-hanging branches, and then straightened suddenly. He stiffened, and Kylie cried out.

"Will!" Walker yelled as he ran.

"Walker! Stop!"

Will turned to the soldier. "No. It's okay. He's a friend. He won't hurt you. He's just concerned for the child. It's okay. We can still go get the vehicle, and you can be on your way."

Will turned his body in such a way as to block the soldier's view of Walker. He wanted all the man's attention focused solely on him. "Listen, all I want is the girl. I don't care about you or what you got going on in the least. I just want to take my niece and get out of here. I will trade you the girl for the vehicle. You can ride out of here. No one has to get hurt."

Will focused on the man's hand. He seemed to loosen his grip slightly. It could have been wishful thinking, but Will thought he was about to put her down.

The soldier tried to look around Will. He was still concerned about Walker.

"Walker. We need a minute. Can you meet me back at the Bertrands? I'm having a conversation with Kylie."

"Will?"

"Walker, please, man."

"Okay. I'll be in the house if you need me."

"Thanks, bro."

"Okay. Now, just lower the knife, and we'll walk out of these woods to the barn. The keys are in it and ready for you."

Will shifted his weight to turn, and the man freaked. He stabbed the knife in Will's direction, shouting something in Chinese. Will was sure the man understood English, but maybe he didn't speak it—not well.

Will lowered his voice and tried with everything in him to sound calmer than he felt. "Settle down. It's okay. I was just going to lead the way. You can go first if you like."

Will bobbed his head nervously and even flashed him a slight smile. He felt an almost sickening wave of relief as the soldier lowered his hand to his side. Will took a step back and held his hand out, gesturing for him to advance. The soldier shifted Kylie to his left side and held the knife out in front of him as he neared Will. As he did, Kylie bit down on the man's loosened hand, causing him to jerk the knife back toward her.

Will launched himself forward, landing hard against them. They all went to the ground. Will's sole focus was on the man's knife. He would do whatever it took to keep him from plunging it into his niece's body. Whatever it took.

~

Will felt the knife graze his shoulder as they struggled for control of it, but it didn't hurt like he thought it should. He jabbed his elbow into the man's rib cage as he wedged himself between the soldier and Kylie. "Run, Kylie! Run to your mom!" he yelled. But she couldn't. Her leg was pinned somehow. He could feel her tugging. He shifted, thinking he was the one holding her down. As he did, he loosened his grip on the man's wrist and felt the steel of the blade on his forearm. If it cut him, he didn't feel it. It didn't matter. All that mattered was freeing Kylie so he could get her back to his sister and her siblings where she belonged.

She tugged one last time, and her leg popped free from the tangle of the men's legs. She shot to her feet immediately and began screaming for Savanah. Will thought of Cayden and Isabella as he listened to her voice fade as she ran away. He was spent. He was malnourished and dehydrated. Just running to get there had zapped all his strength. It had been a miracle that this young, strong, Chinese soldier hadn't overcome him already. Will was resigned to his fate. But still—he couldn't give up. It wasn't in his nature. He'd promised Melanie he'd keep Cayden safe. And Cayden was anything but safe at the moment.

Will felt hands pulling him backward. The soldier's eyes widened, and then a look of resignation washed over his face. Will heard the boom of the rifle's report a second after seeing the pink mist.

Mr. Bertrand stepped into view. "You better get the hell out of here before his compatriots come looking for him. I'm sure they heard that shot."

Will stared down at the foreign soldier as Walker pulled him to his feet. Somehow he knew that was not the last dead Chinese soldier he'd see. They'd made it across the Intercoastal and were here at their doorstep. How long before they were in Shreveport or Texarkana? Would Arkansas be far enough away from the fighting? Would they need to push farther into Missouri, maybe even as far north as Iowa? Surely, the fighting wouldn't make it all the way to Iowa. If it did, the whole country would be lost.

Will looked back. "Aren't you coming?" Mr. Bertrand was still staring down at the soldier. His shotgun now resting in the crook of his arm.

"No. Momma and me are going to sit this one out."

Will wanted to turn back and convince him, but there was no time. His family was likely already on the move—or at least they should be. He wasn't even sure he had the energy left to catch them.

"You kids take care, and may the good Lord bless your journey," Mr. Bertrand said.

TWELVE

Isabella

Isabella heard Kylie screaming as she ran toward them. She side-stepped around Jason and then Pete looking for Will, unsure what had the girl so frightened. Cayden stepped around her and took several steps toward his cousin.

"Where's my dad?"

Kylie didn't answer him.

The boom of the shotgun caused Isabella to jump. In seconds, she was running toward the sound, yelling Will's name. She felt arms wrap around her, lifting her off her feet. "Let me go. I have to get to him." Isabella twisted and struggled in Jason's powerful grasp, but he held firm.

"You aren't armed, Isabella. Wait here. Pete and I will go. Stay here with the others." Jason lowered and released her. "Get them out of here," he called as he ran toward the Bertrands' place.

Cayden took off after him. Isabella yelled his name, but he ignored her. She looked back. Savanah had scooped up her daughter and was rounding up Keegan. The others were rushing toward the gate. It was like Black Friday at Walmart. Children were knocked down, and bags were dropped in the panic. "Stop!"

76

Isabella screamed. "Stop! We have to stay together. Just stop by the gate. We need to stay in our groups."

She heard a loud whistle blow. A few in the back stopped and turned. "Just stop. Get into your groups. Parents, grab your children. We need to move fast," Savanah yelled.

She handed Kylie to Kendra and picked up Keegan. The four moved quickly toward the crowd. Isabella rushed in behind them and grabbed a little blond-haired boy dressed only in a soiled diaper. She couldn't see his mother anywhere. Isabella hoped she had her other two children with her. They didn't have time for tracking down any more kids. Their time had run out. That shot had to have meant that the enemy had arrived. Will would never have fired otherwise. It would attract unwanted attention.

People paused and waited for slower members of the groups to catch up, and things looked much more orderly as they turned out onto Sugar Cove Road. The sun was high overhead, and their shadows were short on the pavement as they quick-walked west toward the Sugar Hill community. They'd turn before reaching it and cross Jeremiah Guidry's field, a shortcut that would take half a mile off their trip. It wasn't much, but with the number of miles they would need to cover each day, every step saved would add up.

Savanah had pushed herself to the front of the pack and was setting the pace for the groups. That would have been Pete's son's job. Pete's wife, daughter, and grandchildren were among the families in the front group. Beau wasn't with them. Isabella hadn't seen him take off after Pete and Jason. Where was he? Where was Rob? The whole plan seemed to be falling apart. They'd practiced for weeks. Everyone knew what to do. But the plan relied on certain members to be there to lead the way and to scout ahead to secure safe resting places. Was that where August and Rob were? Had they gone out to survey the route ahead of the community? That was the plan, right? Her mind was going fuzzy on the details now. All the stress was getting to her as the reality of the situation set in.

Isabella couldn't help but look over her shoulder continually.

Her mind went to all kinds of bad places as she waited for a glimpse of Will and Cayden. She was kicking herself. She should have run after Cayden. Will would have wanted her to stop him, but he was with Jason and Pete. They were armed. He'd be all right.

Will is okay. They are all fine. They had to be. They'd all catch up with them at the first rally point.

Isabella couldn't imagine her life without Will and Cayden. She'd only known them for two months, but there was something about an apocalypse that brought people together in a closeness that she'd never experienced before. If something happened to them now, how could she possibly go on? This new world was so harsh and difficult. Life without Cayden and Will would not be a life.

The group would rest there in the big white barn before crossing the interstate and pushing north. Will would meet her there. They'd go north together. She had to believe that.

Isabella's right arm was burning from holding the toddler. She shifted the boy to her left hip as her eyes roamed the group for his mother. Finally spotting her, Isabella quickened her pace to catch up. The young mother's frightened eyes appeared to look straight through Isabella, and then slowly, she registered her son's face. The mother stopped walking and gasped. Her mouth dropped open and formed an O. Her eyes widened, and she lowered the child she held to the ground, snatching the blond-haired boy from Isabella's grasp, and squeezing him tight to her chest. The child began to cry, and she spoke softly to him. Her gaze returned to Isabella.

"I cannot begin to tell you..." she began.

"No need. You have your hands full. I'll take this one." Isabella reached down and took the tiny hand of the little girl clinging to the young woman's leg. She yanked her hand away and wrapped her arms around her mother. She was no more than three years old and much too heavy for the woman to carry them both. "It's okay, sweetheart. I just want to hold your hand while we walk. We'll stay right here next to Mommy."

The child looked to her mother questioningly. The mother nodded, and Isabella took the girl's hand in hers. They continued walking, picking up the pace to catch up with the rest of the young woman's group, which consisted of another family with small children. The wife held a child on each hip, and the father had a little boy on his shoulders.

Isabella and Will had talked about the perils of moving the group north. Traveling with small children had been difficult even when there'd been motorized transportation, and was overwhelmingly hard under the current circumstances. They'd be forced to move much slower than would be prudent normally. The parents, who were likely even more exhausted than Isabella, couldn't carry the children very far before needing to stop to rest. But with the current threat, Savanah wasn't allowing for breaks. She was pushing them hard and fast, wanting to put as much distance between the group and the enemy soldiers as possible.

The members of the group who didn't have children were taking turns toting the kids to give the weary parents some relief, but it wasn't enough. They'd traveled less than two miles, and everyone was breathing through their mouths and having difficulty keeping up with Savanah. She had to have been as exhausted as the rest of them, but she was driven to keep moving. Isabella imagined that the weight of her new responsibilities as group leader propelled her.

Her right shoulder was hurting now. The little girl kept tripping over her own feet and yanking on Isabella's arm. Isabella picked the girl up and placed the child on her right hip. She didn't protest, slowly lowering her head onto Isabella's shoulder and in seconds, her head lolled and rolled back and forth with each step Isabella took.

The pain in Isabella's shoulder moved up to her neck and down her back. Her legs were heavy, and each step was labored. She was quickly running out of steam. Pessimism dragged her emotions down into a dark place. The reality of the situation was overwhelming, and the hopelessness of their chance of making it made it that much more difficult to keep putting one foot in front of another. She felt the sweet child's warm breath on her neck and felt a pang of guilt. She couldn't give up already. The children needed her. The parents needed her. Will and Cayden needed her to be strong.

This is a mind game, Izzy, she could hear Jaz saying. They'd been workout partners. Jaz had helped her to push through the pain many times.

It's won or lost in your head, girly.

Oh, how she missed the fiery girl now. Isabella doubted she'd ever see Jaz or Gus again. She'd never know if Jaz's baby was a girl or boy.

Get out of your head, Izzy.

Jaz was right. The game is played in the mind. She was no quitter. She'd push on harder and faster. Will and Cayden would meet them at the barn. They'd all rest there and then move north to safety.

Pete will lead us to Texarkana. We can do this. It won't be easy, but we can make it—all of us. We'll make it to safety.

No surrender, Izzy.

THIRTEEN

Will

Will spotted Pete heading towards them as he and Walker reached the Bertrands' barn. "No! No! He should be leading the group away right now. What is he thinking?" The only thing holding him upright was Walker's arm around his waist. His energy was spent, and his legs weak beneath him. His heart was still racing as adrenaline coursed through his body from the fight with the Chinese soldier. How could he push on? He was nothing but a burden to them at this point. At that moment, Will could understand how the Bertrands felt.

Maybe I should stay with them.

"Pete and the others must have heard the shot," Walker said.

"There's no time. He should have headed in the other direction."

"The rest of the group will be on the road already. You can guarantee that Pete and Jason would've made sure of that as soon as they heard the weapon being fired," Walker said, shifting to take more of Will's weight upon himself.

"What happened?" Pete called from across the open field.

Jason and then Rob came into view behind him.

"Enemy soldier," Walker called back. "We need to double-time it out of here."

Pete cursed loudly and continued toward them.

Will was trying his best to walk on his own and not lean so heavily on Walker who he could feel slowing. None of them were in any condition to be carrying one another. Will dug deep within himself, trying to find the strength to move his legs faster, but came up empty. His thighs felt like wet noodles.

He looked past Jason and drew in a deep breath. "Cayden! Dammit! What are you doing? You should be with Isabella and Savanah on the road getting the hell out of here."

"I had to find you."

This was all wrong. Nothing was going to plan. Everything Will had done to try to ensure his son's safety was failing. He was failing.

Jason rushed toward Will and took him from Walker with Pete on the other side. They moved quickly back across the field toward Sugar Cove Road. Will kept looking back to make sure that Cayden and Walker were able to keep up. They had to stay together.

As they passed Savanah's farm, Will was relieved to see that everyone had left already. Since he couldn't see them on the road, that meant that they'd crossed the field near Sugar Hill and were on their way to the rally point. There were weapons, supplies, and food at the barn. They'd set up sandbags and created firing positions to defend the place. There was a safe place fortified with steel panels for the children to hide. All they had to do was make it to the barn and wait.

"We're going to cut through the Johnsons' place. It will save us twenty minutes," Pete said. "You have to watch for booby traps. Old man Johnson used to make moonshine, and he was a paranoid old cuss."

"I'm all for saving steps," Will said as Jason and Pete led him down the Johnsons' gravel drive.

Pete stopped abruptly. It took Jason a second to realize and halt himself, causing him to jerk Will's injured shoulder. Excruciating pain shot through him, bringing with it a new wave of nausea. Pete slid out from under Will and pulled his rifle to his cheek. He scanned an area near a weathered and leaning shed.

"What is it?" Will asked.

"I saw movement."

"It's probably just a cat. Mrs. Johnson had tons of barn cats. The untamed ones have been hard to catch. Will shuddered at the thought of what people had had to resort to in the face of starvation.

"No. This was much bigger than a cat. It moved back into the shadows of the shed. Wait here. I'm going to go check it out."

"I got your back," Rob said, falling in behind Pete. The two men slowly crept across the lawn toward the junk-strewn shed one hundred feet from the back door of the Johnsons' home. An equally weather-beaten wooden barn was to their right, surrounded by now unoccupied corrals and pens. The weeds had all but taken them over.

Walker and Cayden slid in to assist Will, and Jason joined Rob and Pete. "We should take care of those wounds while they go check things out," Walker said.

Will stared back at him. "Wounds?"

"You're injured, Dad." Cayden pointed to Will's shoulder and his eyes followed his son's finger. Indeed, his left shoulder was soaked in blood. He followed the trail down his arm, where more gashes told the story of his struggle to gain control of the soldier's knife. Will felt a wave of nausea at the sight and choked back the bile rising in his throat. He wasn't normally so queasy at the sight of blood. Maybe he'd lost more than it appeared.

Walker pulled him toward a porch along the western side of the Johnsons' Acadian style house. He lowered him onto one of the steps made of native cypress, dropped his pack, and was about to grab the medkit when they heard shouting.

"Hands in the air. Let me see your hands," Pete was yelling.

Will's mind immediately assumed more Chinese soldiers. He stiffened and reached for the knife in his pocket, all while pulling Cayden close to him. He was not going to let them get close to his son.

"My hands are up. They're up, man," a male voice said in perfect English. There wasn't even a hint of Chinese in its tone. Will's shoulders relaxed, and he loosened his grip on Cayden's neck. The man wasn't Chinese. He was American.

"What are you doing here? What do you want?" Pete asked the man.

"I got shot. I'm shot, man. We were chasing down two enemy combatants and got into a firefight when we caught up with them. I took a bullet to my left leg."

"Two?" Pete asked. "Where are they?"

"I don't know. When my team and I got close, they started firing. I took a round and crawled in here. My team took off after them. I heard screaming shortly after they took off, but no shots were fired."

"The booby traps," Jason said. Pete nodded.

"Should we check it out?" Jason asked.

"They're heavily armed. We need to avoid trouble if at all possible," Pete replied, staring off toward the back of the Johnsons' property.

"You're sure it was only two enemy soldiers?" Jason asked.

"No. I only saw the two, but there were a shit ton of rounds coming at us. We were holding off a unit of enemy combatants back on the highway. A small team of them broke through our defenses near the crossroads and took out some of our guys. We set off to stop them from flanking the rest of our unit."

"So there's a team now?" Pete asked.

"There was a team. We took out all but two—maybe three."

Will stood on wobbly legs and took a step toward the shed and the men. Walker caught him by the arm before he fell, and he and Cayden helped Will over there.

The soldier was just a kid, really. He looked barely old enough to shave, yet he wore their country's uniform and had been injured in battle defending her. He was thin and dirty, and blood oozed from a wound in his left calf. Will spotted another wound near his neck. Walker dropped his pack to the ground next to the kid and pulled the medkit from its pouch. Pete continued to question him as Walker cleaned his wounds and bandaged them the best he could.

"How did the Chinese get this far into the country?" Jason asked, standing over the kid with his rifle still at the low ready position.

"We just don't have enough ammo—or warm bodies. We've lost a lot of soldiers. Some left to get their families the hell away from here. Some died from sickness. My sergeant was convinced that the Chinese were using biological weapons on us as men started falling like flies. It could have been biologicals. I don't know. When we got the order recalling us to Fort Polk, we were all relieved. Until we realized that we were not being replaced—but retreating and giving the enemy ground—US ground. It's still unfathomable." The kid shook his head. "If we'd only been able to get resupplied, we could have held them off and pushed them back into the gulf."

"What's the plan now?" Jason asked.

"Plan? I don't think the brass has one. The Chinese are on our heels. Even if we were able to make it back to base and get resupplied, we'd be fighting them there within a day."

"How many?" Will asked.

"A shit ton," the kid said, his expression grim. "A battalion, at least. We heard that another was moving up Highway 87 toward Shreveport to cut off our resupply from Texarkana."

"Are there troops in Texarkana?" Will asked.

"That's the rear operating base for Fort Hood's command. They are reinforcing the refugee shelter. It's all screwed up. Nothing is being done according to regulation. I'm not even sure who the hell is in command anymore. There have been very limited communications."

"That's messed up," Pete said, rubbing his salt and pepper goatee.

"Why Texarkana? What's strategic about there that the military would set up a command center there?"

"The rail lines and Red River Army Depot. Also, it's close to the Red River," the soldier replied.

Pete bobbed his head and then glanced back at Will. "I can see that. You guys live around here?" the kid asked.

"We live along this road," Jason said.

"I'd be getting my family out of here if I were you."

"We are. They're on their way to Shreveport and then Texarkana though," Pete said.

"Shit!" the kid cursed.

"We have to stop them," Will said.

"Where else are we going to go, Will?" Pete said, turning to face him.

"I don't know, but it's not safe now."

"Nowhere is safe, man. The Chinese are coming in like locusts, and there is very little we can do to stop them. All we can hope for is to slow them down and allow residents time to evacuate north."

"North Arkansas? Or north, as in Canada?" Will asked.

"Canada is under the control of the Russians, so that's out," the kid said flatly.

Will's heart leaped into his throat. "Russians?"

"Yeah. It was a coordinated attack. The Russians, North Koreans, Iran, and China worked together to pull this off. How else would they have taken down the most powerful country on Earth?"

All Will's optimism about finding a safe place to stay and survive this mess evaporated in an instant. How could they possibly survive this? He reached out and pulled Cayden close. Melanie's voice whispered in his ear. *While there is breath in your body, protect our son.*

"We'll find a place—somewhere," he whispered. He wouldn't give up. They would never surrender.

FOURTEEN

Will

Will's mind raced as they left the young soldier back at Johnsons' farm and hurried to catch up with their families as they pushed north to escape the advancing enemy. No longer was he under the illusion that they could quietly make their way to the safety of the refugee camp in Texarkana. Gone was the idea that they could take their time finding a place in which the group could set up a new camp of their own in the woods of Arkansas and live off the land. He could see how foolish the plan was now. Even without the advancing army, living off the land was nearly impossible. How could they possibly feed forty people by roughing it in the woods and hunting? What a fool he'd been to think they could. He'd trusted Pete and believed that whatever skills were necessary for survival could be taught before leaving Texarkana. What alternative had there been? He'd needed to hold on to any shred of hope.

What hope could he find now?

If the young American soldier was right, the middle of the country would soon fall under communist China's rule. They'd be forced into work camps, barely fed, and tortured. Was that their fate? How could this have happened? If they hadn't been so busy killing each other off and fighting over what little resources they had, the average American citizen would have been a mighty force against the Chinese.

It wasn't like there was a shortage of guns and ammunition around. There were still plenty of weapons and though ammunition was a problem, crates and boxes full were likely sat in warehouses and on trucks somewhere out there. But that did them no good right now.

"We need to fight back," Jason said, breaking the silence that the group had fallen into on their trek. "We're retreating when we should be standing our ground and fighting."

Rob stopped in front of them and turned back. "We have families. What do you want to do? Put children on the front lines with sticks and slingshots?"

"We can't protect them by running either. It's only a matter of time before they control everything. Do you want to see your little ones in some concentration camp learning Chinese?"

"Would they be fed?" Rob's stare was hard. Will couldn't believe he'd even consider it.

"They may not want children. They may only want able-bodied workers," Will replied coldly.

Rob's mouth parted as if he was going to speak, and then he turned to look away. "What are we supposed to do? We aren't soldiers. We don't have weapons for war. We barely have enough bullets to hunt, let alone fight an army." He choked on the last part as if he were about to break into tears.

"We'll have to use guerrilla tactics," Pete said, pulling his rifle closer to his chest and allowing it to rest in the crook of his arms. "We'll have to set ambushes and use what we can find to slow them down—take out as many as we can." A smile tugged at the corners of Pete's mouth. Will had learned that Pete had been practicing for something like this for years and hoped he wasn't itching for a fight just to prove something.

"We have to form our own army," Jason said. "We have to convince people that they must fight—or die."

"Maybe we should join with the regular military. I bet they'd give us weapons," Cayden said.

Will considered it for a moment. They'd no doubt be recruiting. The kid soldier had said they'd lost a lot of men and lacked warm bodies to do the fighting, but they didn't have supplies or ammunition.

Will shifted his weight onto his left foot and faced Jason. "Are you thinking about Tank and the others back in Vincent?"

Jason nodded. "And Valson and the folks of Sugar Hill."

Will bristled at the mention of Valson, recalling with vivid detail the scene when Jason's family had held him hostage. "You've seen him then?" Will asked.

"I know where he's holed up. He could convince Sugar Hill to join us."

"Why would they?"

"Because they have families in there to protect too. We have a common enemy."

"What about our families?" Will asked. "Savanah's is no longer safe. The enemy is crawling all over there by now."

"We could stay at the rally point near Perkins for a week at least. We have enough supplies. We could head to Leesville and cut off the advancing Chinese—find a way to stop them. When it's safe, we can have our families push on to the next rally point near there. The grocery store at Roseville would do for a few weeks—maybe even a month. There's good deer hunting within ten or fifteen miles of there. If we got a few of them, we could hold out there while we pick off as many of the enemy as possible."

"You talking *Red Dawn*-type tactics?" Will asked. He'd seen the original movie with Patrick Swayze. A ragtag bunch of kids taking on the Russian army made for good fiction, but the Chinese carried real weapons, and it didn't end that well for Patrick Swayze's character in the end anyway.

"It could work," Pete said.

Will tried to picture how it could succeed. In the end, he determined that they didn't really have a choice.

～

Will and the others reached the barn that acted as their first rally point just before sunset. The group was there and safe for the moment. The relief Will felt at seeing Isabella's smiling face was palpable. Savanah looked like she'd aged a decade in the few hours since he'd last seen her as she stroked her braids and paced as Keegan ran to greet Jason. She should have been relieved to see them, but her stress level remained high. After a long hug and kiss, he pointed to his sister. "Is she okay, Izzy?"

"No, not really. She did fine all the way here. She led the group and kept everyone moving, but as soon as we arrived, the reality of the situation hit her. She didn't want to stop. She urged everyone to keep going and put more distance between us and the Chinese but the parents refused. They just couldn't keep on carrying the heavy packs and their children.

"I'm glad they didn't. We've sort of had a change in plans."

Isabella's eyes grew wide and she stepped back and crossed her arms. She looked down and then back toward Pete and the others. "What happened back there?"

"Kylie didn't tell you?"

"She said a bad man grabbed her and that you knocked him down. We heard the gunshots, and Pete said to get moving."

"It was a Chinese soldier. Our military was chasing three scouts. He got separated from the other two."

"Are you all right?" She touched his blood-soaked sleeve.

"Just a graze," he said. It was more of a gash, but he didn't need to worry her about it.

"What about the other two Chinese fighters?"

"We ran across one of our soldiers. He was wounded. He filled us in. The rest of his team went after the other two. That was when the plan changed." He took her hand and pulled her close then placed her hand on his chest and looked into her eyes. "We aren't going to be able to outrun them." She gasped and held her breath. "Our military is depleted and can't hold out much longer. The Chinese are running up the border with Texas on their way to Shreveport. We might already be behind enemy lines right here at this barn."

Tears pooled in her eyes and his heart broke at having to tell her the bad news. Looking up, he surveyed the group and found Savanah. She was bending over, rummaging through her pack. How would he possibly make her understand? She had four children to protect. All she wanted in the world was to get them to safety. She wasn't easily going to accept that they'd need to stay put, make a stand, and use every opportunity to thwart the enemy's plan to run up the middle of the country. No, she would never understand that. He wasn't sure he did himself.

Isabella placed her head on his chest and squeezed him tight. "Are you sure? Really sure?"

"We're going to go have a look for ourselves, but the soldier had no reason to lie."

"We can't fight an army! We don't even have ammunition!" Her voice was pitchy. She was about to cry. He'd give anything to prevent that, but the reality was, they were in serious trouble.

"Pete has some ideas, and Jason plans to involve my cousins and the people at Sugar Hill. We need every able-bodied adult to resist this, or we could all end up in Chinese camps."

"No!" Isabella said. She lifted her head and took a step back. "That can't happen."

"We are going to resist, Isabella. We won't surrender. This is our country, and we have to fight to save it from them."

"Will," Jason called.

"I have to go. We're going to take a trip over to Merryville and see what we can learn. Pete has a cousin over that direction. We hope to recruit him and his family into our scheme."

"I don't like this, Will. And Savanah is going to freak."

"I'm going to let Jason tell her. I think she'll take it better from him."

"Coward," Isabella said, a smile tugging at her lips.

Will bobbed his head. "Yes. Yes, I am."

FIFTEEN

Will

MERRYVILLE, BEAUREGARD PARISH, LOUISIANA

They arrived at Pete's cousin Josh's house by midday. They'd barely had any rest since they'd left the homestead. Will hadn't slept more than a couple of hours before Pete had tapped him on the shoulder and told him it was time to go. They'd packed very few provisions, wanting to travel light though Pete had produced energy bars and MREs, citing the importance of the mission and the need to move quickly. Will felt guilt taking them from the rest of the group. Every morsel of food was precious, and what he took for himself would mean a mother or child might not eat soon. Food was a constant worry for everyone. No matter how much time had passed, Will had not become accustomed to being constantly hungry.

Blank stares looked back at Pete as he filled Josh in on all they'd learned about the Chinese army's movement north. Josh's wife pushed herself away from the round oak table opposite their tiny kitchen and stood. She steadied herself for a second and then ran from the room down a short hall. Will heard her vomiting. That was exactly how he'd felt when he learned about it. It was a hard thing to grasp. Even though they'd known for a couple of months that this could happen, that it actually was happening didn't seem real.

"You didn't come all this way just to tell us this," Josh said.

"We can't run from them. It's too late for that. I thought we'd have more time, that we'd hear that they had broken through down by the Intercoastal, and we'd have time to bug out, but that didn't happen, and they are up here already and pushing north rapidly."

"So? What's your plan?"

"We have to fight. We have to make a stand and stop them if we can," Pete said with conviction in his voice.

"How do you propose we do that, Pete?" Josh's wife asked from the doorway.

"Just the way we trained, Lorraine."

She scoffed. "That was play-acting, Pete. We were preparing to defend homes from a few marauders, not an army."

"We aren't going to take on a whole army. We're going to disrupt them and pick them off one by one. Remember the divide-and-conquer strategy we trained on. Diversion and subversion."

She shook her head. "That's crazy talk. They have modern weapons of war. You aren't going to sneak up on them. You'll never get close enough to use that big ole tactical knife you carry. You're fooling yourself if you think this plan of yours has a chance in hell of working.

"We only have to slow them down," Jason said.

"Slow them down?" Josh asked.

"We need to slow them down so that we can slip past them and make it to Texarkana," Jason replied.

"We're not going to no camp," Lorraine said with her hands on her hips. "We talked about this, Pete. You're the one that said that the FEMA camps would be bad. We'd have to give up our guns and might even be separated."

"Do you have ammo for your guns?" Will asked. A shot of hope coursed through him. If they had even a few boxes, it could help.

"Not much. We have some shotgun shells and rounds for the thirty-thirty for hunting small game," Josh said.

Will's hope faded. A shotgun would only be useful to them up close. It would make a good defensive weapon if they were cornered by the enemy, but they needed ammo for their rifles so they could pick off bad guys from a distance and race away. The goal was to figure out who their top-ranking soldiers were and take them out. And to take out any communications equipment they had. They also needed to get their hands on enemy weapons. Explosives were their main goal. They could do a lot of damage to the Chinese army's movement if they had just a few explosives.

A knot formed in Will's gut. The more they talked, the more his stomach churned. The plan did sound crazy. They'd all likely be killed, but someone had to try to stop them. Someone had to make a stand. Could they sit back and allow them to just roll through the country and not fight back? The answer was no for him. Each person would have to come to that conclusion on their own, but for him, he would not surrender his life and freedom to an enemy occupier. He was willing to do whatever it took to make sure his family didn't have to either.

"Who is left around these parts?" Pete asked.

Josh glanced over at Lorraine. "Cain and his family left last week. Lorraine's brother is still here. His wife's family is about three miles north of here. Really..." He paused and turned back to Pete then took a deep breath and exhaled. Most folks around here are dead already. Those who weren't killed in the initial days and weeks after the lights went out have died of hunger—or suicide." He swallowed hard and then continued. "Those damn Chinese won't find many people to resist them. In my mind, that was their plan all along. They just waited for us to all die off so they could roll on in and take the land for themselves."

Will agreed with him. Even those that had tried to flee had been cut down by the marauders and road warriors. He had no way of knowing how many residents had actually made it to Texarkana. They may get there and find a nearly empty camp.

"So, what are you going to do now?" Pete said. "You going to sit here and wait for them to round you up and put you all in camps —or kill you here?"

"Hell, no!" a young male voice shouted.

Will spun around in his chair. Behind him stood a teenage boy of maybe sixteen. His hair was stringy and greasy, and his clothes dirty but his dark eyes were fierce with intensity and conviction.

"We're going to fight, right, Pop?" He moved around the table and took a stand behind his father. "We ain't cowards, Uncle Pete. We ain't going to let no foreigners steal our country."

Will's eyes dropped to Josh. He was expressionless. Will couldn't tell what he was thinking but was sure that he was proud of his son. Tears welled in Josh's eyes and he stood. "Right, son. We're going to fight those MFers and push them back past the bayou and run their asses into the gulf."

"Now you're talking, cousin," Pete said, moving around the table and smacking Josh on the back. He held out his hand to the boy, and they shook vigorously. "All right, now let's round up the rest of the folks around here, and go make them pay for invading America."

The kid picked up his red MAGA hat and placed it on his greasy head, wiped the sweat from his brow, and hitched up his baggy jeans. A smile spread from ear to ear. "I'm ready. I know my friends are too. We've been sick of sitting around and doing nothing."

Will envied the youngsters who had gathered in Josh's shop to talk strategy with Pete. He counted twelve. Seven boys and five girls. All between the ages of fourteen and twenty. They looked better fed than the adults. Four of the boys had Armorlite style rifles slung over their backs. Two of the girls wore pistols in holsters at the hips. They looked like sisters.

The adults that Josh and Pete had rounded up sat around the firepit in the backyard. Jason was working hard to convince them of the soundness of the plan. Will didn't blame them for their apprehension; he had a teenage son and there was no way he'd want him taking up arms against an army. He knew it would come to that, eventually though; he couldn't see a way to avoid it. Everyone would have to fight if they were to defeat the enemy.

"Roadblocks? Really? That's the best you can come up with?" one of the men asked.

"We want to funnel them into an ambush," Jason replied.

"Why wouldn't they just use some of that heavy equipment they have to push the cars and tractors out of the way?"

"They likely haven't had time to move equipment like that through the bayou. Our army blew up all the bridges across the Intercoastal before they were able to move much more than their troop carriers across."

"How do you know that?"

"Our contacts down at Lake Charles. They sent word when the military blew the remaining bridges. We thought that would be the end of it, but they'd already sent some troops across," Jason said.

Will hadn't thought about the bridges in weeks. It would take time for the Chinese to move equipment north now, and what about their resupply? Would they have the same issue that the American Army was having with supplies reaching them? How long could they hold out?"

Will moved from the doorway of the shop toward the group gathered around the firepit. "We need to cause them to use up all their ammo and find a way to steal or destroy their food and water. They won't have a way to resupply. They can't just go out and get more. It's not available for them to find. They will be as defense-less as we are. That would give our army time to resupply and get here to wipe them out."

"That's what I was planning for," Pete said behind him.

Will turned. "I'm not thinking clearly. I missed the part about them not getting resupplied."

"It's okay, Will. We're all running on empty. We need to fuel our bodies and stay hydrated. We have to be fit and ready for battle."

Will knew he was right. He needed to eat as much as his body required and stop feeling such overwhelming guilt about it. It was as necessary as putting fuel in a car. Without it, it would not operate. His head felt fuzzy; even a few calories would help clear that up. He reached up with his left hand to wipe sweat from his eyes, and pain shot through his shoulder. The image of the Chinese soldier's expression as his knife sliced Will's arm flashed before him.

"So, we just need to cause them as much trouble as possible and wait for their supplies to run out," Will said, lowering himself into the lawn chair next to Jason.

"It will be a little more complicated than that, but pretty much," Jason said.

Scenes from the movie *Red Dawn* played in his mind as he prayed their story had a happier ending.

SIXTEEN

Savanah

PERKINS, CALCASIEU PARISH, LOUISIANA

The thirty-foot by fifty-foot metal building near the barn was filled with tools, equipment, and worn-out furniture that looked to have been taken from someone's elderly parents' home, complete with the doilies left on top of one of the chests of drawers. If they were going to remain there for very long, they would need room to spread out.

The old, weathered wood barn wasn't big enough for living in. Families were tucked away in every corner. Every stall was occupied by parents and their small children. The single men occupied the loft also acting as lookouts. Everyone was taking turns on watch. Tensions were running high, and nerves were frayed beyond anyone's ability to cope. Jane had even snapped at Kylie who'd looked as if she'd been slapped. Savanah understood perfectly. Jane was pregnant, and between the morning sickness, the mood swings, and the overcrowded conditions, her patience had run out.

"What are you thinking?" Jane asked from the doorway of the metal shop building.

"I'm thinking we need to have everyone grab something and move it out so we can make room for people in here. Some of the furniture could stay. It would give you and the other mothers a place to rest comfortably. Maybe I could even get Keegan and Kylie down for regular naps."

"That would be something," Jane said forcing a smile.

"This is tough on everyone. The kids are pushing boundaries because they are stressed too."

"I know but they're fine. They're tough, like their mom. They'll do fine." Jane turned. "I'll go round everyone up. We'll have this space livable before the guys get back."

Savanah sighed. "I keep hoping that they'll come back with good news, and we can get back on the road to Texarkana."

"I know; me too. I don't want to have my baby in a barn. They'll have doctors and maybe even drugs at the shelter."

Savanah just nodded. She doubted seriously that they would have either—not with a war waging to their south. All available medical personnel and pain medications would be needed on the front lines. Mothers had delivered babies since time began without either, but Savanah understood Jane's concerns.

It took the better part of the afternoon on their third day there to remove enough stuff from the shop building to begin making decent living quarters for the group. The single men remained in the loft of the barn, and any items from the group's packs and bags that they didn't need right away stayed behind in the barn.

Savanah spread out Keegan's and Kylie's sleeping pads and bags between hers and Kendra's. Karson's was placed to block them in so they couldn't go wandering off in the night.

Everyone's mood seemed to be improved with the extra room. Luca and another man hauled water in five-gallon buckets from a nearby pond to flush the toilet which was a wonderful luxury after days of using the woods behind the barn.

"Mom, Jane found a large pot in that junk we hauled out of

here. She's wondering if it would be all right to start a fire and boil some rice for everyone," Kendra said, poking her head through the large roll-up door.

Savanah chewed on her bottom lip as she replayed Pete's instruction in her mind. No fire was at the top of the list. The smoke can be seen and smelled for long distances. It could alert people to their presence. "No. I'm sorry. No fire. The smoke will give us away."

"Even a little one—just enough to boil water?" Kendra questioned.

"Even a little one. It just isn't worth the risk. We can soak the rice."

"It never gets soft that way."

"Put it in the sun. It should warm the water some."

It was a fairly warm day for December. They'd left the roller door and the walk-thru door open to allow a breeze to blow through the shop but Savanah was still sweating.

"Okay. I'll tell her. She's not going to be happy."

"I know, but we have these rules to keep everyone safe."

"I wish we didn't have to stay here. Why can't we just move at night when we can't be seen?" Kendra asked.

"Because we can be seen by the Chinese military. They have night vision equipment. Besides, don't you think they could hear us coming for miles?" Savanah looked to the children playing loudly in the corner.

"I guess you're right." Kendra slowly turned to go and then stopped. "Are we safe here, Mom?"

Savanah swallowed hard before answering her daughter. "As safe as we can be."

Kendra sighed and exited the building without another word. She knew. She knew they weren't any safer there than at their homestead. That was one of the reasons Savanah regretted letting Jason and Will talk her into this mess. They wouldn't be safe until they reached Texarkana. That couldn't happen soon enough for her.

~

Jason, Will, and the others returned just after dark. Pete was smiling and headed straight for his wife. Jason was expressionless; Savanah couldn't read him. Will—he looked sick, like all the air had been sucked out of his lungs. Savanah was afraid to ask what they'd discovered. After the string of bad news they'd received lately, she was sure this was the worst kind.

She greeted Jason with a kiss and he took her hand in his. "Are you okay, Will?" she asked, her tone low. Cayden and Isabella arrived as Jason began to tell her what they'd discovered on the scouting mission near the Texas-Louisiana border.

"There was a steady stream of military vehicles moving north along Highway One Eleven. It would take a sizable army to stop them. We talked to Pete's cousin in hopes of at least slowing them down and we have a plan. Josh and his family are implementing a critical part of it now. We wanted to come back and let you guys know. We're going to move to our secondary location at the store in Roseville."

"Does that mean we are staying put for a while?" Isabella asked.

Jason's head bobbed, and Savanah's heart sank. The grocery store had been cleaned out in the first few days after the lights went out. The owner had placed three-quarter-inch thick plywood over the windows, but thieves had somehow smashed down the door and broken in. The shelves were completely bare, but it was big enough for the group to remain together.

"What about the town?" Savanah asked.

"We didn't see anyone the last time we checked. It looked like everyone had evacuated already," Jason said.

The scouting teams had cleaned out the walk-in freezer. That would be used to protect the children in the event of an attack. They had installed a lock on the inside of the door and Jason assured her that it would hold. She still wasn't comfortable with being locked in the windowless space. If the town was deserted, they only had marauders and the Chinese to worry about but she took very little comfort in that thought.

"So far, the Chinese appear to be leaving civilians alone," Jason said.

"That will all change when you start making trouble for them. They'll likely respond by hunting us down and killing us all," Savanah said.

"They won't connect us with you guys. We won't lead them back to you. Once we initiate contact, we'll stay until it's finished."

Savanah shuddered. Jason reached out and touched her shoulder. "After we disable them, we can all get back on the road and make our way to Texarkana. Pete's cousin said Texarkana is heavily fortified and well guarded. The Chinese army will avoid hard targets like that. At least that's what I'm thinking."

"Why are they aiming for Shreveport then?" Isabella asked.

"I'm not sure of the strategic importance of the city, but there must be one because they are racing to get there."

"What about Fort Polk?

"The rumor is that the army has retreated and abandoned the base. They've been called up to help secure Texarkana."

"Doesn't that mean that they've given up on driving them out of Louisiana?"

"That could be the case. I know the soldier we spoke to said they were out of supplies and ammo. Their resupply never came. Maybe they're waiting for a shipment before they can get back into the fight."

"You really think there's going to be another shipment?"

Jason said nothing.

Savanah looked to see if Will was going to comment. He looked out of it. "Will, are you sure you're okay?" Savanah asked, sidestepping Jason and heading for her brother.

"Actually, Sis. I think I could use one of your herbal teas. My stomach and head aren't feeling all that great," Will replied.

Isabella reached up and felt his forehead. "You do feel warm. It could just be the heat, but it could be fever too."

Savanah walked over to him and placed the inside of her wrist on his forehead. He did feel a little warm. She hadn't brought many herbs with her, thinking she'd find what they'd need along the way, but she did have some echinacea and rosehips. That might help boost his immune system.

"Dad, how's the cut to your shoulder healing."

Savanah looked sideways at her brother then peeled up his left sleeve to reveal an angry-looking gash. "Dammit, Will. This is infected. Why didn't you let me clean it when it happened?"

"We had enough to worry about. It was just a small gash," he said defensively.

"And now that small gash is oozing pus, and you're going to need antibiotics!" She was steaming. It was irresponsible of him. They needed to reserve the antibiotics for as long as possible. Savanah stormed off toward the field behind the barn where she'd seen some comfrey and had planned on cutting it to take with them. She'd need it now to make a poultice for her dumb brother's stupid arm.

"I'll come with you," Isabella said. "I need some air."

She sounded as pissed off as Savanah was. She was sure Will was going to get an earful later when they were alone.

"I can't believe he let that happen again," Isabella said.

"Again?"

"We've both dealt with infected wounds. Things were quite nasty in Houston after the hurricane. We had battle wounds that got infected. He should have known better than to ignore a cut."

"I think the lack of food is causing us to make mistakes. Potentially deadly mistakes," Savanah said.

"You think we should return your homestead, don't you?" Isabella said as they picked the comfrey leaves.

"I've thought an awful lot about it, Isabella. It just seems senseless to wait here. We aren't any safer. In fact, we're less safe, even at the store with the sandbags and steel bars Pete installed inside the freezer to hide the children."

"We have to believe that this new plan will work," Isabella said.

"Do we?"

It was a crazy plan. They could all get killed. What would they do if Will, Jason, and the others never came back? No one had an answer for that. This was new territory for all of them. None of them had ever had to navigate a world where their homeland had been infiltrated by a foreign power. She knew that Jason, Will, Pete, and the others were doing their best, but what if their best just wasn't good enough? How would she keep her children safe?

"You ladies need some help?"

Savanah turned as Walker approached. "Yes. I could use some help to convince Jason and the others that we need to return to the farm."

"I think they have their minds made up on that point, Savanah. I know Pete is preparing to go after the Chinese and put a monkey wrench in their strategy to cruise through the midsection of the country and he isn't going to be persuaded to set aside his plan. Not now. Not when he's got people willing to fight back. I understand you're concerned about the children. We're all going to do our very best…"

"No matter how hard everyone tries, you can't stop bullets, and we can't outrun an army." Savanah fought back the tears.

"No, we can't, but that army makes a lot of noise, and it's difficult for them to move without attracting attention. If Pete and the others can keep them tied down long enough, this plan of theirs might just work. At the very least, it will put a hurting on them and decrease their numbers."

Savanah didn't believe it for a moment. She shook her head, turned, and walked away without a word.

SEVENTEEN

Will

MERRYVILLE, BEAUREGARD PARISH, LOUISIANA

Will wasn't feeling one hundred percent yet, but Savanah's treatments seemed to be working to curb the infection in his left arm. When Will and the others arrived back at Pete's cousin's, Josh, Lorraine, and the others had the roadblock ready to be set up. Two tractors had been found with enough fuel to move vehicles onto the roadway along the enemy's route. The US military had managed to delay them south of Ragley. According to the scouts sent that way, a few Chinese units had broken through and would arrive at the roadblock by dark.

Would they move after sunset? Will guessed that would depend on how much of a hurry they were in to get to Shreveport. It was still a mystery to him why they would be heading there. Maybe they could capture one of them and find out.

"Is everyone in their places?" Pete called out.

Each two-person team relayed that they were. Josh and two other teams had crossbows and arrows trained on the road. Pete and his son were the only ones with rifles, so they covered the rear. They would take out anyone trying to retreat. Will felt useless with his shotgun and two shells. He had to continually dismiss the fact that what they were attempting was downright crazy based on the reality that they had to try. How could they do nothing? This was their country. If they didn't stop the enemy, who would?

The convoy of five Chinese Dongfeng armored military vehicles arrived an hour before sunset. The communist army hadn't been expecting resistance. If they had, they would have sent out a patrol to make sure there weren't any roadblocks. They rounded a bend in the road and halted abruptly two hundred feet in front of the ten or so cars and trucks blocking both lanes of Highway 111. They just sat there for a moment before soldiers in the rear vehicle dismounted and made their way along the ditch toward the road-block. Will heard the tractor start. A second later, he heard a rifle's report echo through the trees. There was no way to tell if it came from Pete or the enemy. Then more gunfire erupted. Pete was returning fire. Will could tell it was him by the sound of the three-round bursts instead of the steady rounds of the automatic rifles. The gunner in the last vehicle began firing. Rounds tore through the trees, splintering wood and kicking up dirt.

Will strained to see if the tractor made it onto the roadway. He could see the big green machine rolling forward, but it was much too slow to have been moving with intention. The automatic gunfire continued, but the machine kept rolling. Eventually, it reached the roadway but stopped short of blocking both lanes.

From where Will stood next to the trunk of a large oak tree, he could tell that the driver had been killed. He was slumped over the steering wheel. The rear vehicle began moving backward at a high rate of speed. It swerved into the opposite lane, nearly missing the tractor. As it did, the next vehicle in the convoy followed suit and then the next. They fired into the woods on both sides of the road as they backed away. All Will could do was press his body as close to the ground as possible and pray.

The group had succeeded in causing the convoy to detour but

had failed in their attempt to ambush them. There was only one road for them to take to head north. They'd have to go west for a couple of miles. Before they reached their turn, they would encounter another roadblock and another attempt at an ambush. Jason, Rob, and the teens would be waiting for them there.

After the last vehicle disappeared from view, Will rushed toward the tractor. Pete was already there, along with Josh and Lorraine who was cradling an elderly man's head in her arms and sobbing uncontrollably. Josh was rubbing her back and attempting to console his wife. It was a heart-wrenching scene and stirred up emotions in Will as he recalled losing his wife. He pushed through the grief that tried to pull him down and walked past the couple to where Pete and Beau were standing. On the ground at their feet was a soldier. Will looked into the man's eyes as he stood over him. He was so young. Fear framed his face. Here he was, bleeding out on a highway in America, far from his homeland and his family. He likely was only following orders. At another time, he could have been a tourist here to enjoy Mardi Gras. They could have sat down and had a beer together and talked about baseball. Now, they were enemies because his communist ruler said so. It was so pointless.

"He's not talking," Beau said.

The soldier coughed, and blood spurted onto his chin and ran down his neck. It looked like a round had struck him under his armpit. It likely went through his right lung. With Pete and Beau being positioned in the trees above the road, the bullet would have traveled toward the ground and injured vital organs.

Will knelt beside him. He picked up the kid's hand and squeezed then leaned down and whispered, "I'm sorry this happened to you. We did not want this. We are fighting for our lives here." The kid's eyes shifted toward Will. He understood.

Maybe not the words, but the tone in which they were spoken. "I can't help you with your wounds, but I can stop your suffering. It can take a long, long time to die and be very, very painful." He left the words to linger. The kid closed his eyes slowly and then opened them. "I can help you if you help me." The kid's eyes shifted to the right, away from Will. He was rejecting betraying his country.

"I say we leave his ass here to die a slow and painful death," Beau said. He took two steps forward and nudged the soldier with the toe of his boot. "I wouldn't spit on him if he was on fire." He spat a few curse words and walked away.

Will released the kid's hand and let it fall to the pavement. "Have it your way." He started to stand and felt a hand brush his arm. "Knife," the young soldier managed to get out.

"You want your knife?"

He moved his knife up and then down slowly.

"I want to know why your military is rushing to Shreveport? What is there that you're so interested in?"

The kid moved his head from side to side.

Will stood and backed away. "You got nothing for me. Then I can't help you."

A few seconds passed, and then Will heard the kid whispering.

"Airbase," the soldier said softly. "Airbase."

"An airbase? What about it? Planes aren't flying, are they?"

"Doomsday," the kid said before going into a coughing fit.

Will knelt beside him once again and wiped the blood from his cheek. He gently rolled him onto his side slightly to help clear his mouth and throat. "Doomsday? What the hell is that?"

Pete stepped closer. "Are you talking about the president's Doomsday plane?"

Will's eyes shot up at Pete. "The president?"

"The fleet of E-4Bs are called Doomsday planes due to their function as a survivable airborne command post for the president. He can initiate a nuclear strike from the plane."

"Could the president's Doomsday plane be in Shreveport?" Will asked.

"It's possible," Pete said. They both stared down at the soldier. The PLA sure was in a hurry to get there. If that was the case, they had to do everything in their power to stop the Chinese from getting to Shreveport. It could be the country's only chance to come back from this thing.

"We need to go help Jason and the others. We have to stop the convoy at all costs," Will said, rising to his feet.

As the two men walked away from the soldier, Pete nodded over his shoulder. "What about him?"

"He's not going anywhere," Will said.

It was a long night as Will stared at the back of the Dongfeng, stopped at the second roadblock. The other team had stopped the convoy by blocking them in with a road grader and dump truck. The Chinese soldiers hadn't attempted to dismount their vehicles or ram the heavy equipment. They occasionally fired rounds from their turrets but seemed to be just popping off warning shots. Will hadn't seen movement for hours. Were they waiting for reinforcements? How long would they wait inside their vehicles? It had to be obvious to the occupants of the vehicles that his group didn't have the means to force them out. Will wasn't sure if even an RPG would do the trick. The People's Liberation Army's version of the Humvee was likely as heavily armored as the US version.

Sometime before daybreak, a runner came bearing news from the battlefield to their south. Another convoy with ten vehicles was heading in their direction. Did the soldiers here have a way of communicating with the rest of their unit? Probably.

"We need to send folks back to the main roadblock to intercept them. We can't let them break through the roadblock or reach this team here."

"We need a way to blow them up," one of the teens said.

"Like an IED?" another kid said.

"Yeah."

"Anyone know how to make one?"

"My cousin does," a lanky teen with long greasy hair replied.

"Wait. What?" Will asked.

"My cousin makes IEDs. Pipe bombs."

Will turned to the kid next to him. "Go get Pete. He's going to want to hear this."

While the teen repeated what he'd told Will, Pete's eyes brightened and a smile spread across his face. "Alrighty then. Let's get him up here."

"He's on his way to Texarkana."

"That's not helpful," Pete said, turning to leave.

"He's got pipe bombs in his shed though."

Pete whipped back around and rapidly approached the kid. "What?"

"Yeah. He showed me. It freaked me the hell out. I wasn't sure if they were safe. He said they didn't have the detonators and showed me where they hooked in the wires on the bombs."

"You know how to activate them then?" Will asked.

"I don't know. He just showed me that one time."

"You're sure he still has them in his shed? Where does he live?" Pete asked.

"About a mile from here," the boy said.

"You're sure that the bombs are still at your cousin's house?" Will didn't want to go off on some wild goose chase. He was exhausted already and barely had the energy to stand.

"I'm sure. I asked him about them a couple of weeks ago. He said he was afraid someone would go rummaging through the shed looking for food or valuables and find them, but he didn't want to move them. He didn't want his parents to find out."

"We need to get a team and go check this out," Pete said.

The lanky teen led them through the business section of a small town to a residential area of older homes. It appeared that the town had been evacuated. No one came out to investigate them.

"Which one, Levi," Pete asked as they stood in the intersection staring down a tree-lined street.

"The third house on the left." Levi pointed to a small home with bright yellow shutters. It looked like the homeowners had tried to plant a garden in the front yard, but whatever food might have grown there was long gone now. Will's stomach growled at the thought of a lovely ripe tomato or perfectly delicious carrot. He could almost taste them. He shrugged off the thought of food and followed Pete and Levi toward the side of the home. In the backyard was a portable shed secured by a keyed lock.

"Do we need bolt cutters?" Will asked.

"We don't have time to track a pair down. We'll kick in the door," Pete replied.

A moment later, Pete did his best to get into the shed via the door. After two kicks, he had to rest. Levi took a turn, and within a minute, he'd made a hole in the plywood door big enough to crawl through.

"Be careful picking up the pipes. We have no idea what's inside them," Pete admonished.

Will's butt puckered every time the kid appeared in the hole with one of the short sections of steel water pipe containing some explosive mixture that could potentially blow them all up. Pete gingerly took the pipe bombs from Levi and placed them on the grass next to the shed. Will couldn't help but wonder what in the world the kid had been thinking to make bombs like that. What had he intended to do with them, blow up his school? He'd likely got the plans on the internet. Will hoped that he'd closely followed the instructions or they could be the ones blown up by them.

"We need something to carry these in. Will, look around for a crate or something," Pete said as he took their future IEDs from the boy.

Will looked around the sides and back of the shed but found nothing. After a search of the rest of the yard, he ventured into the neighboring yard and found a milk crate.

He stopped near a pile of trash and retrieved a discarded towel to provide some cushioning for the bombs. Pete then placed the pipe bombs down into the crate and covered them with the towel.

"How are we going to detonate these?" Will asked.

Pete pulled back the towel and lifted one end of the pipe. "See that small hole?"

Will nodded.

"The fuse is inserted there." He picked up a small plastic grocery sack, rummaged inside, and retrieved a bundle of wires. He reached in again and pulled out a switch.

"Bridgewire detonators."

"Seriously?" Will asked.

"This kid was seriously deranged," Pete said.

"How did his parents not know?"

Pete stuffed the items back into the bag and handed them to Levi.

"His folks were high most of the time. They couldn't care less what he was doing as long as he wasn't bothering them," Levi explained.

Will shook his head. "Sad."

"Let's get these back and kick some ass," Pete said.

"You think these will work against those armored vehicles?"

"Your guess is as good as mine. It's the best shot we have, so I sure hope so. Something has to end our Mexican standoff. We'll have to give them something to shoot at to coax their gunners out. If we can get their gunners to expose themselves, we have a shot at taking them out. Without their heavy machine guns, we can get close enough to place these devices."

"We should put some on the road leading to the roadblock," Levi said.

"No. We don't want to take the chance of them going off-roading and bypassing our roadblock altogether, but pre-positioning them within the kill box in front of the roadblock is an excellent idea."

Will couldn't stop thinking about Cayden and Isabella back in the town they'd left them in. He knew that Savanah would be doing her best to make a comfortable place for everyone and hoped that all their preparations had made it a safe one as well. With Pete, Jason, Rob, and others here fighting the Chinese, their families would be forced to fend for themselves if trouble found them. It had been a difficult decision, but Will was sure that going to fight was the right one. With the new information he'd gained from the wounded Chinese soldier, he was even more sure that anything they could do to interrupt the PLA's plans would make a difference. He was also anxious to get to Shreveport and find out for himself if indeed the US president was there and if there was some semblance of government left in the country.

"What did you make of the information about the Doomsday plane?" Will asked as they made their way back to the roadblock.

Pete stopped and leaned against a tree by the edge of the road. He wrapped a hand around the nape of his neck and rubbed. "I pray he is telling the truth and that the government is still active and doing something to save this country. I know that one of the Air Force's E-4Bs transports the secretary of defense to foreign countries. I recall reading that the military was planning on upgrading the fleet but I'm not sure if that happened after all the defense spending cuts of the last administration. The president had proposed massive spending to rebuild our military, but that takes time to implement."

"It makes sense that something of that importance would prompt the PLA to rush to Shreveport. What other strategic importance could the city have?"

"We likely will never know, but we can do our part and hold them here as long as possible. My hope is that our military will show up and finish the job for us. I'm not sure how many of these things will actually work, to be honest." He nodded to the crate of pipe bombs on the ground next to his feet.

"So, if the president or some member of the government is on a plane and heading to Shreveport, what does that mean? Is DC gone?"

"My guess is it does. Retaliatory strikes would have been made on the countries suspected of taking out our power grid. Nukes could even have been employed."

"Nukes?" Levi asked, his voice pitching.

"Almost certainly. We have ships out at sea capable of launching if we are attacked. I wouldn't be surprised if Beijing and other countries' capitals were hit with nukes," Pete said.

Will tried to imagine what that might do environmentally. It would suck to succeed at repelling the invaders only to die of radiation poisoning. He imagined it would be a slow death, though, ending in cancer or something since they hadn't been in a nuclear ash cloud or anything.

Pete picked up the crate and sat it on his hip. "I bet we'll find out that the whole East Coast is wiped out once we get to the FEMA shelter. Hopefully, someone there is a gossip, and we can find out some inside information. I doubt they're sharing much in the way of detail with the general population."

So much of the plan was now up in the air. Will hated not knowing what life would look like when they arrived at the shelter. Life might be totally different in other parts of the country. They could learn that the Midwest was spared or the West Coast. They could be evacuated to someplace with electricity and running water. He'd never allowed himself to hope that before.

"Doomsday plane," he said under his breath. It could change everything. "Please, Lord, let there be a government out there somewhere with the ability to save this nation."

EIGHTEEN

Isabella

ROSEVILLE, VERNON PARISH, LOUISIANA

While Will and the others set off for Beauregard Parish, Isabella and the rest of the group made their way north to Roseville. They'd twice had to detour their route to avoid gangs on the road, but safely made it just before dark on the second day. After settling everyone in at the grocery store, Isabella and Walker patrolled the town.

Resting her bat on her right shoulder, Isabella continued down the street back toward the grocery store. She'd been on patrol for a little over an hour, walking the four-block section, and felt confident that they were the only people in the area. She stopped at the corner and listened. It was eerie to hear near-complete silence. There wasn't so much as a dog barking. She was used to the lack of mechanical noises now, but rarely did she get far enough away from the others to hear silence. Even though they'd been taught all about noise discipline by Pete and his family, it was impossible to enforce with babies and small children.

She glanced across the street toward Walker, her patrol partner. He held his bat out in front of him, ready to pounce if needed. She was grateful that he'd stayed behind to help protect the group though there wasn't much that could be done if they were attacked with much force. They had very little ammunition for their guns, only the walk-in freezer to be used to protect the children.

The good thing was that most of the groups that did roam the streets looking for prey were also unarmed—at least with anything with bullets. There were a plethora of knives, swords, and other sharp weapons. One of the women in their group carried a bow and arrow. She was a good shot and even brought them back a squirrel once, but she only had a few arrows left, so it wouldn't be useful in a fight with numerous attackers.

Walker pointed to the street on their left, and Isabella turned and walked down the south side of the street. Walker cut across the intersection and walked along the north side of the street. Isabella glanced at the store windows as she passed. The gift shop and art supply store looked untouched. There must not have been anything useful for survival inside. Next to the flower shop was a dress store with bridal dresses on display. Isabella slowed and admired the gowns. She imagined herself wearing one on her wedding day. Will would be in his black tuxedo and Cayden in a shirt and tie. She couldn't help but think about how different their lives could have been if not for the stupid war. When she turned her attention back to patrolling the street, Walker had pulled ahead of her and was just reaching the next intersection. She double-timed it to catch up with him.

He stopped and turned to look back. A shot rang out and Isabella jumped, barely recognizing the sound. When she did, she dropped to the ground and crawled to a space between two buildings. She prayed that the others back at the store had heard the shot and were taking action now to protect themselves.

"Walker!" she cried out.

She heard no reply. Isabella stretched forward, taking the risk of being shot to see if she could locate him. She spotted him pressed up against the wall of the building on the corner, his only cover the wall of the entrance to the shop. "Walker," she called again. He held up a hand and gestured for her to stay put. She desperately wanted to know where the shot had come from and how many attackers there were, at the same time fighting the urge to run away. Running could get them killed. Where would she go? She could go back to the store but she might lead the shooter there. If she ran away, she'd be separated from them and may never see Cayden or Will again. She couldn't bear the thought of that.

She waited for what seemed an eternity before the shooter revealed himself.

The gunman, dressed in a sleeveless T-shirt, shorts, and cowboy boots, slowly inched forward from the side of the building just twenty-five feet from Walker. In his hands, he held a rifle on a sling around his neck. He either had plenty of ammunition or was an idiot. He was obviously not a good shot. With a rifle like that, and aimed in Walker's direction, he should have hit him. Isabella had heard that the marauders who roamed the area were drug-seeking, mostly. They were strung out on prescription painkillers and other drugs they'd found in homes while moving from town to town.

Walker must have been listening to the man's footsteps. When he was within striking distance, Walker leaped from the alcove and smashed the bat down hard on the man's arms. The rifle dropped and dangled on its sling as the gunman screamed in pain, clutching his broken arm to his chest, and hopping around.

Walker slammed into him, knocking him to the ground. Before Isabella could reach them, Walker had disarmed the man and was standing pointing the rifle at the man who was still writhing on the ground in pain, complaining about his arm.

"Shut up. You deserve to have every bone in your body broken for shooting at us," Isabella said. She pointed her bat at the man. "You better shut the hell up, or I might just test this thing out on your shins."

The man's eyes grew wide, and he looked away. "I'm sorry. You scared the hell out of me. There ain't supposed to be nobody left in town. The mayor and everybody left two weeks or more ago.

"Are you from here?" Walker asked.

"No. My sister lived here. She had a house over on Fourth Street. I was going to stay there for a few days."

He raised his hand to wipe his nose, and Isabella jumped backward with her bat held ready to strike.

"I was with a group, and they were getting on my nerves, so I thought I'd crash here for a few days to pull myself together before pushing on to Shreveport. I was going to try to hook up with my sister and the rest of the folks from town here."

"You strung out?" Walker asked.

The man looked up. "I'm hurting real bad."

"When's the last time you used?"

"Yesterday."

"You say you left this group voluntarily?" Walker asked.

Isabella was trying to understand why Walker was giving the man the third degree about his drug use. What did it matter now? He wasn't going to arrest the man for drug possession, was he?"

"Yep. I got tired of those assholes. That leader—he's a prick. He was always bossing me around, telling me I had to go find booty for the group to earn my keep. I ain't nobody's bitch. I go where I want when I want."

"You sure they didn't kick you out?" Walker asked. "You sure they didn't follow you here to this town?"

That was what he was getting at. Now, Isabella was concerned. Walker was on the right track. If they were after this guy, her group could get in their crosshairs.

"No. They didn't see me leave. I waited until everyone was asleep. They were passed out cold when I slipped away."

Walker handed the rifle to Isabella who took it and stepped back, aiming it at the man's head. Her finger found the trigger, and then she placed it resting just to the side of the trigger guard. She was shaking so hard that she was afraid she might pull it by mistake.

Walker bent and patted the man down, checking the pockets of his jean shorts and stepping back. "Where is it? In your drawers?"

"I ain't got nothing on me."

"Where did you stash it then?" Walker asked.

The man drew in a breath. He'd stashed it.

"Oh my God. They're coming after you for drugs, aren't they?" Isabella said, the realization hitting her like a ton of bricks.

"It's mine. I earned it. They had no call to treat me like that," the man whined.

"Show me!" Walker said, hauling the man to his feet. He shoved him forward, causing the man to stumble. Walker caught him and pulled him into the intersection.

"Which way?"

"I..."

"Which way?"

He lowered his head, resigned that Walker was not going to give up. "It's in that stack of tires beside the tire shop."

"Let's go."

Savanah paced back and forth, stopping in front of the man several times. She looked like she wanted to kill him. He sat on the stool with his head bowed.

"He'd better be praying," Isabella said under her breath.

She scanned the room. The stares of angry parents would have made her wet her pants if she'd been him. She wasn't sure if she'd rather have taken her chances with the marauders. These folks looked like they were ready to tear him from limb to limb. Isabella understood how they felt. This man had put their children's lives in danger. She glanced back at Cayden who sat on the floor with Kendra and Karson, his arms folded across his chest; he felt the tension rising. She wanted to go to him and take him away from this place, but she had no idea how to find his father. She wondered what Will would do in this situation. What would Pete do?

She was pretty sure she knew what he would do. His wife had already suggested it.

"Take him out and dump him beside the road out on the interstate. They'll think he overdosed or something, and then they'll have no reason to come here."

They weren't killers. Isabella doubted that anyone here was to the point that they could do something like that even to save the group. But they could run him out of town. He could go east. Would they still trace him to the town? She couldn't be sure.

The door banged open, and everyone jumped up.

"They're here!" the teenage girl yelled.

NINETEEN

Savanah

Savanah had her back to the door when it banged open. Her first thought was that she had a rifle trained on her back. She spun around, searching for her children. Kendra and Karson were sitting with Cayden.

Where are Kylie and Keegan?

And then she remembered. They were with Jane and Luca inside the walk-in freezer. The door was latched tight, and they were both armed. The little ones were safe.

She barely registered the words from Rebecca. Pete's daughter had been one of those sent to watch the road into town. She was breathless and sweating. She'd run all the way. How much time did they have? Minutes? Could they hide from the vile group heading into town?

"What about him?" Jack asked.

Jack had only recently moved to Sugar Cove Road. Savanah hadn't known him all that long, but from what she knew of the man, he was an honest and hardworking sort. Her grandfather would have liked him. Jack been injured in a fight defending his family and his broken leg had healed badly. He walked with a limp and was in constant pain. He couldn't run. None of them could. They'd have to hide. They would fight, but only if forced to.

"Tie him up. We can't have him alerting them. If they search for him and don't find him, maybe they'll think he carried on through without stopping," Walker said.

Walker and Jack gagged and restrained the man, placing him in a closet in a back room. With the boards on the window, the gangsters wouldn't be able to see in, but Savanah wasn't taking any chances. She moved everyone to the back stock room. Everyone held their clubs and bats. Some held knives and others machetes. Walker stood in the doorway with the man's rifle.

"How many rounds are left in it?" Savanah asked.

"Two."

"That's two more than we had this morning," she said, trying to be optimistic. Walker smiled.

She drew in a deep breath, attempting to calm herself. It didn't work—not at all. She could hear the children crying through the walls of the freezer. If she could hear them, could the bad guys outside?

In the corner, a mother and teenage daughter prayed, holding on to one another. Her teenage son was still out there. He was on the lookout two blocks away. The drug gang hadn't made it that far yet. Once they reached the boy's position, there would be no other option for him but to stay put.

Savanah prayed the gang would turn and head east or west before reaching town; it wasn't likely. There was a chance that they wouldn't search the store. If they found it locked, would they assume that the drug addict wasn't inside? She was grasping at straws now. The waiting was torture. She felt like a trapped animal as she took her place between Kendra and Karson. Cayden was next to Isabella. They were holding one another. Savanah thanked God for her. Isabella loved Cayden like her own. It was plain to see she'd defend him with her life. Will was so blessed to have found her.

"We need to quiet the children," someone whispered.

Savanah turned. It was Francis. He'd joined the group only a week before they left the homestead. Will had found him barely breathing and dehydrated while out on one of his patrols. Savanah hadn't had much interaction with him, but what she'd had wasn't all that positive. He wasn't a big fan of children. The boy had hooked up with the wrong group. But he was right. The crying could alert the bandits to their position.

"I'll see what I can do," Savanah said, releasing her daughter's hand. As she drew near to the door of the freezer, she recognized the child's cry immediately. That was her child—her *problem* child.

"Jane. Luca. It's Savanah. Let me try to calm her."

Jane yanked open the door and thrust Kylie into Savanah's arms. Kylie cried louder when she realized it was her mother. Savanah rushed her down the short hall and into the bathroom. She dropped to the floor and pulled Kylie into her lap, took her by the shoulders, and looked her in the eyes.

"Kylie Jane, you have to stop that crying right this second. You hear me. There are bad, bad men on their way here, and if you don't stop crying, they could find us and hurt us." Her eyes grew wide, and she quieted to a whimper. "Do you understand me, Kylie? You could get hurt if they find us."

She didn't want to frighten her daughter, but Kylie's world revolved around herself so Savanah needed to make it personal to Kylie. Big tears streamed down her pale cheeks. "You are safe inside the freezer with Jane and Luca, but you have to be very, very quiet. Okay?"

"But they won't let me play with the jacks," Kylie whined.

She was seven and very bright, therefore intelligent enough to grasp the seriousness of the situation. Savanah couldn't understand why the child could not control herself. She wished with everything in her that her grandmother was still alive. She would know what to do with Kylie. Savanah was nearing the end of her patience. Nothing she did seemed to make any difference to Kylie's outbursts or behavior. Before, it was just her. She could deal with it, but now, it was putting the whole group at risk. She sighed heavily, stood, then took Kylie's hand and led her out into the manager's office.

"Sit." Savanah pointed to the office chair. Savanah opened several drawers before finding what she was looking for. She held it up. "What's that for, Mommy?"

Savanah handed the roll of duct tape to Kylie. "You are going back inside the freezer, and if you cannot control yourself…"

Kylie took it and jumped up from the chair. "Okay," she said, heading back toward the freezer.

Jane looked shocked when Savanah explained. "If she makes any more noise, use the tape."

They waited in the backroom for ten or fifteen more minutes before a knock on the back door came. The last two lookouts had spotted the marauders. They were heading straight for downtown. Savanah's gaze fell to the man who'd brought them there. She narrowed her eyes. A part of her wished they'd taken Pete's wife's suggestion and left him dead in a ditch. Guilt pricked her heart, and she asked for forgiveness but if anything happened to the children, the man was as good as dead. The parents would see to it.

They could hear glass breaking in nearby buildings both at the front and the rear of the store. It sounded like they were just being destructive for the fun of it. A loud thud came from the front of the store and then another. Savanah's heart leaped in her chest, and she felt Kendra squeeze her hand.

"It's okay. They can't break through the plywood."

"What about the doors? Are you sure the steel bars will hold?" Kendra asked.

"Jason was sure."

Kendra's grip softened. Oh, how Savanah wished he was there now. She hated that he was so far away and there was no way to communicate with him. Before, just months ago, everyone took for granted that you could pick up a phone and call practically anyone in the world.

Another thud sounded, this one louder and sounding like boots on metal. Someone was kicking the door. Walker moved into the hall where he had a clear line of sight of the door. He raised the rifle to his cheek and aimed. Savanah moved into the doorway, holding her bat ready to defend the others. They would have to go through her to get to them. She prayed the bars on the door held. She prayed with all her might for her children's protection.

"Smoke!"

"What?" Savanah said, whipping around to face the room.

"I smell smoke," Jack said.

"Oh my God," someone yelled.

Savanah rushed past Walker toward the rear service door. "Watch them. I'm going to check the back."

The steel bars were still in place, but the smoke was seeping in under the door and around the sides. Someone had set a fire outside the building. They were going to be smoked out. Savanah felt the steel door. It was cold. She ran her hand along the wall. It was cool to the touch. She rushed back and pulled the door to the storeroom shut.

"Wait! What about the fire?" Jack asked.

"It's just smoke. I don't think the building is on fire. I'm shutting the door to keep the smoke out. Stay put. I'm going to check out the front of the building."

"I'm coming with you," Walker said.

As they ran toward the front of the store, Savanah could already tell that the gangsters had set fire to the front of the building. Heavy black smoke hovered near the ceiling. Savanah covered her mouth and nose with her shirt and ran toward the door. She placed her hand on it, then yanked it away. The front of the building was burning. How long did they have? She looked at the ceiling. Not long. The smoke would get them before the flames. Panic seized her throat. She tried to swallow but couldn't. She couldn't think straight. She had to get her fear under control. She had to figure out how to get everyone out without being seen.

Walker felt the glass windows. "They're pretty warm."

"What do we do now?" Savanah asked.

"We need to know where they are. We'll have to find a way out without them seeing us."

Walker ran to the back service door and began removing the steel bar across the door.

Savanah ran back and felt her way to the manager's office. There was a small window near the ceiling that wasn't covered in plywood. Maybe she could see out and discover where the attackers were. She pushed and shoved, finally moving the desk under the window. She climbed on top of it and stood on the tips of her toes to look outside.

"See anything?" Walker asked as he entered the room.

All she could see was the building across the alley. "The warehouse's doors are partially open. If we could slip out the back doors, maybe, just maybe, we could go through the warehouse and escape on the opposite street." She strained to see if anyone was near the doors then thought she heard talking outside. She moved to the side of the window and listened.

"They'll have to come out eventually," a gruff male voice said.

"We don't know how many of them are even in there, Ralph. They could be heavily armed. We just don't have enough information for this," another male voice said.

"Walt said to get them out of there. You gonna go questioning his orders?"

"No," the other man said.

"But I don't like risking my life just to capture some teen chick."

Savanah gasped, and her hand flew up to her mouth. They'd spotted the girl she'd had on lookout and followed her here.

Dammit! She'd screwed up. She should have just hunkered down here. She had no idea what the hell she was doing. She was a homesteader and mother. She sold herbal teas and candles for a living. She was no soldier. She wasn't a fighter, but she needed to become one—and quick.

"Can you tell how many are back there?" Walker asked.

"It sounds like just the two men."

"We can take on two. If we can do it quietly, we could get everyone into the warehouse," Walker said.

She climbed down from the desk and made her way to the storeroom. The others needed to know. They couldn't make this decision on their own.

"The front of the building is on fire. The flames have not breached the walls, but the store is filling with smoke."

There were gasps and groans. "Shhh," she said. "We have to be quiet. We can't let them know where we are in the building."

"They're going to kill us all," one of the women cried.

"At least two men are waiting out back here. We may have to fight our way out." More crying erupted from the group. Savanah held up her hand to quiet them.

"Savanah and I are going to attempt to take out the two men while you all get the children and get out," Walker said. "There's a warehouse across the alley. The doors are open."

Some were shaking their heads. They were frightened. Savanah understood that. "We have to do this. We have to get the kids out."

"Find your way out to the side street. I think it's Eighth Street. Run as fast as you can west. Turn north on Pine, and there is a community center on the corner of Pine and Eleventh Street. The side door on the north side of the building is unlocked. I checked it yesterday. Go there. Wait as long as you can for us," Walker said.

Savanah's eyes searched for her children. Kendra and Karson were holding hands. Isabella was holding Cayden's and Kendra's hands. Her eyes met Isabella's. Isabella nodded. She knew what was on Savanah's mind, and she acknowledged it. Isabella would take care of her children if she didn't make it to the community center. She'd find a way to get them to Will and Jason. She was a strong and capable woman.

Walker motioned toward the door. "Everyone line up. We're going to go tell Jane and Luca. Everyone needs to grab a kid."

When the door to the freezer opened, Kylie ran to her mother. Savanah felt to make sure the tape was secured across her daughters mouth then thrust her into Isabella's arms. "You need to hold on to that child for dear life. Do not let her make a sound."

She knew the child that posed the greatest risk of exposing them was her own. She closed her eyes and prayed that Kylie would behave. "Just this one time, Lord. Please let Kylie not be defiant."

"I'm going to throw open the door. We're going to jump out and confront the two men. When we do, you race across the alley," Walker said.

It sounded so simple when he explained it, but nothing ever was. The men were likely armed. Maybe with pistols or rifles—at the very least, knives. The chances of taking them out quietly were next to zero. Despite the odds, they had no choice. She would not hand over the girls to those perverts. They would likely kill the children and men. The fate of the women and girls would be worse than death. She would never let that happen to Kendra and shuddered at the thought of those vile men touching Kylie.

TWENTY

Will

All Will could think about on their trek back to the roadblock where the rest of their team were waiting for the communist military to arrive were the two words they had gotten out of the Chinese soldier. His urgency to get to Shreveport was intensified a hundredfold since learning that the presidential Doomsday plane could be there. If it was, that meant that some form of the government was still operational. He wanted to know what was being done to win this war and return the nation to its former condition. He needed to know. The toll this mess was taking on the citizens was enormous and would require strong leadership to bring it back from the brink.

Pete was ahead of him by a few paces. He stopped and slowly lowered the pipe bomb-filled crate to the ground.

"You really think those pipe bombs will explode?" Will asked.

"Right now, I'm not taking any chances. When we get them there, I pray at least one does."

The plan was as weak as his legs felt. They were playing a game of Russian roulette. With every step Will took, that fact became clearer in his mind. He just hoped that by slowing the invaders down, they would be giving the government, or what was left of it, time to complete their mission in Shreveport or to secure that plane and its occupants—if indeed it still existed and was in Shreveport. There was just so much unknown. Would anything they did make any difference? Absent any other news, all they could do was try.

"It was mid-morning when Will, Pete, and Levi arrived back at the roadblock. Pete had everyone move back to a safe distance as he and Will placed the IEDs along the side of the road, inside a pothole and under one of the cars in the roadblock. They ran the wires along the ditch and into the woods to a large fallen log. That was where Pete would be located. He insisted that he was the only one qualified, even though he had no experience with bombs. Will didn't argue. Part of him felt guilty for that. All he would have had to do was flip the switches. It wasn't complicated. Pete had already inserted the bridgewires and set the switches.

"When the blast goes off, be ready to fire as soon as anyone exits a vehicle. We don't want to give them time to set up and return fire. We don't have the ammo for a prolonged gunfight," Pete told the group.

From his position, Will had a clear view of the "kill box," as Pete called it. He'd be firing on soldiers exiting from the driver's side of the vehicles. Jason was hidden at the front of the roadblock and would be firing down the right side of the convoy. Pete was concerned about overlapping fields of fire and other terms Will didn't yet understand. He felt way out of his element. He was an instrument technician—or had been. He was trained to turn valves, not fight wars. Yet there he was, about to face down foreign soldiers. All he could do was pray that his aim was true. "One shot. One kill," he repeated to himself. "Inhale. Exhale slowly. Squeeze." *I can do this. I have to do this.*

The convoy of armored Chinese military vehicles could be heard a mile off. They were moving fast. No doubt in a hurry to get to Shreveport and the United States presidential Doomsday plane. If Will and the others had their way, these soldiers would never see it. If they were successful, they'd acquire weapons and ammunition today that could be used against the next convoy that tried to come through. Will's group couldn't block every possible route to Shreveport but Will was banking on slowing them down long enough for the regular army to be able to repel any attack in Shreveport. If only they had some way to communicate with their military. Would they welcome the help or tell them to stand down? In the absence of orders, all they could do was what they could.

Will strained to see if Pete was in place as the first Dongfeng rolled into view. He spotted Pete's boots. He was prone on the ground behind the log. Was it far enough away to be safe from the shrapnel? They couldn't even be sure what was inside the pipes. Nails? Ball bearings? Glass? Maybe all three? How far would the shrapnel be propelled? They were about to find out.

The first vehicle halted fifty feet from the roadblock just like Pete had said it would. It was too far for the bomb hidden within the cars blocking the road to have any effect. Will hoped the others did the trick. Pete felt that if even one caused them to have to dismount the vehicles, it would prompt the others to as well. Will hoped he was right and that it wasn't just wishful thinking.

Once all the vehicles had come to a stop, Will stood pressed against the tree, listening to the vehicles' engines, and watching for any sign of doors opening. He waited and then waited some more. The rifle grew heavy in his arms as he trained his scope on the rear vehicle. What was Pete waiting for? Will heard the creak of a door opening and scanned to his left. He saw nothing. A second later, the sound of the explosion boomed and echoed through the woods. Will jumped, startled by the noise, and immediately repositioned himself to obtain a clear view of the driver's side of the convoy. The vehicle in the middle was on fire. Smoke rolled out from underneath it. Pete had blown the IED he'd placed in the pothole.

As soon as the back driver's-side door opened, Will trained his scope on the soldier. When his head came into view, Will inhaled, let it out slowly, and squeezed the trigger. His rifle's report was joined by Jason's and a few of the others posted on the right side of the convoy. It had worked. Their plan had worked. Now they just had to stay alive. The gunner in the second vehicle turned in the turret and began firing in Jason's direction, ripping through the cars and trucks that made up the roadblock. Glass shattered, and rounds tore apart the metal and plastic. When the firing stopped, Will scanned the woodline on the opposite side of the road. Jason emerged with his rifle trained on enemy soldiers on the ground.

Reluctantly, Will moved from the cover of the large oak tree and made his way toward the road. He could see the gunner spin around to fire. Will found the back of the man's head in his sights and followed as he turned. As soon as he stopped, Will trained his weapon on the side of the man's face just beyond where his helmet stopped and squeezed. The communist soldier slumped forward. A barrage of rounds kicked up the dirt and leaves five feet to his right.

Will dove to the ground, rolled, and sat up behind a tree trunk. It wasn't big enough to conceal him, and he doubted it would stop the rounds the gunner in the last Dongfeng was firing at him. He needed to move, but there was no way he could make it back to the large tree he'd previously hidden behind. He was stuck with his back toward the enemy. He shut his eyes as round after round whizzed past him, expecting one to find its target at any second. When the shooting stopped, Will exhaled the breath he'd been holding and sprinted toward cover.

Back at the large oak, he scanned the scene on the roadway. Two gunners were now slumped over their weapons. Will was grateful that someone on the opposite side of the convoy was a good marksman. He wouldn't have lasted much longer. He was sure of that.

He waited for at least ten minutes for more activity, hating the waiting game. Every muscle in his body was tense as he scanned from vehicle to vehicle. In total, he spotted four enemy soldiers on the ground and two more dead in their turrets. Out of the five vehicles, how many more were there to kill? The third vehicle was still smoking, although Will couldn't see any flames. Had the fire penetrated the vehicle? Why hadn't the occupants fled?

Another few minutes passed without a sign of the combatants, then suddenly, all the doors opened, and they began firing into the woods that lined both sides of the road. Will returned fire. He was on his last magazine when the final soldier fell to his knees. Will couldn't see what was happening on the opposite side of the convoy so changed positions and moved to a clump of trees near the back of the vehicles.

He heard one three-round burst and then another, and suddenly two soldiers sprinted toward the underbrush. Will stopped, squeezed the trigger, and fired, but his shot must have been high and missed. Someone, likely Jason, fired, and one of the men went down. The other didn't even look back. He kept going, diving into the foliage, and disappearing. Will ran to where he last saw the soldier and fired into the brush as Jason arrived and made his way along the woodline. He disappeared for a moment before exiting.

"He's gone," Jason said, firing a final round into the man's compatriot on the ground. Will looked north along the length of the convoy. He counted six bodies. The doors to the Dongfengs were open. He and Jason cleared each vehicle and met Pete and Rob on the other side.

"How many got away?" Will asked.

"No way of knowing for sure, but at least four," Pete said.

"Should we go after them?" Jason asked.

Pete pointed to the Dongfeng and then to the soldier's rifle in his hands. "No. We got what we were after."

TWENTY-ONE

Isabella

ROSEVILLE, VERNON PARISH, LOUISIANA

As soon as Walker pulled open the door, the group rushed toward it. They were bumping into each other and fighting for their positions in line. Isabella was holding Kylie as tight as she possibly could. She was bumped into the wall and almost went down, but she held on despite the child's thrashing. She could still hear her screaming beneath the two layers of duct tape. Jane hadn't wanted to take any more chances with the kid. Cayden had his hands on Isabella's back as they exited the building. Kendra and Karson each had hold of one of Keegan's hands. They were together and moving towards the warehouse door. All was going well until Kylie spotted her mother. She thrashed all the more and cried out. The duct tape held, and it was only a muffle. Hopefully not loud enough for the bad men to hear.

Inside the dark warehouse, Isabella slammed her knee into something and let out a curse word. She shook off the pain and rushed to keep up with the others. Jane and Luca each had two children with them and were moving slowly. Isabella wanted out of the dark space. She needed to get past them. As she turned her body sideways to squeeze around them, Kylie arched her back and kicked out. It knocked Isabella back into the wall, causing her to bump her head. Isabella gritted her teeth to restrain herself from swatting the girl. If ever a child needed a good old fashion butt whopping, it was Kylie.

"Stop fighting, Kylie. We need to get out of here before the bad men get us." Isabella grabbed her arm. "Or do you want me to leave you here for them?" Kylie stiffened, and the thrashing stopped as she fell silent. The threat had worked, but Isabella felt horrible. She hated losing her temper with a child. What kind of person was she? She'd have to apologize when they reached safety —to Kylie and Savanah.

The light of the doorway was nearly blocked out by people streaming outside. Isabella waited her turn impatiently. She kept glancing behind them, expecting to see marauders coming for them. When she finally stepped outside, she drew in a deep breath, grateful for the fresh air and sunlight. She hated the dark.

Jack was in the lead and crossed over the street first. He waved them over, and everyone ran west toward Pine. They moved much quicker than Isabella had thought they would and reached the community center in a few minutes. Jack held the door open as the children and teens filed past. Isabella reluctantly pushed through the doorway in search of Kendra, Karson, and Keegan. They needed to stay together. She had to do a better job of keeping them close. She turned down a long hallway that ended in the gymnasium, finding Kendra and her brothers in the corner. She thrust Kylie into Kendra's arms and moved quickly to check the set of steel double doors. They were chained together. It would be difficult for anyone to get in. But it would also be difficult for them to exit the building. They needed to find the key or bolt cutters, just in case.

"I'm going to the office to find the key," Isabella told Jack as she passed him in the hall.

"We need to be able to unlock that door and make a quick escape if necessary."

"The key is hanging just inside the door to the office," Jack yelled after her.

The guys had done a thorough search of the town. They were much more familiar with it than she was. "Thanks. I'll be right back."

Isabella found the key right where Jack had said it would be. She'd removed it from the hook and was turning to leave when she glanced out the office's side window. Movement caught her eye, and she stopped, turned, and waited to see what it was. She thought it might be stragglers or Walker and Savanah but what she saw sent panic through her bones. She dropped down below the window and crawled into the hall then stood and ran as fast as her legs would carry her.

"They found us," she whispered to Jack as she passed him. "I'm going to unlock the door and then tell everyone to run."

"Where to? Where can we go now?" Jack asked.

"Kurthwood. That was our next rally point."

Isabella ran to the door and attempted to insert the key, but with her hand shaking so badly, she dropped it and had to try again. Finally, she was able to get the key inserted, turned, and the lock removed. She shoved open the door, and light flooded the windowless room. "Everyone move now. They've found us. Move quietly. Hurry!" Isabella said.

Jane and Luca each grabbed two children. Everyone else fell in behind them. Cayden held on to one of Kylie's hands, and Kendra held the other. They had her lifted off her feet and she was kicking with all her might. They would need to deal with her. Isabella had to secure the front door and try to hold off the bandits. She had to give the others time to get away.

Jack was there and had already secured the lock. "You go. I got this," he said.

"We should both stay and hold them off as long as possible." Isabella gripped her bat with both hands.

"Let's move to the back door. We'll follow the group and slow down anyone following them."

"Okay," Isabella said.

She watched the others disappear around the corner of a church and turned to see where Jack was. He was gone. She was standing there alone. She turned back, trying to decide what to do when something hit her in the back—hard. It knocked the breath out of her. She fell forward onto her knees, felt hands entangled in her hair, and then she was being dragged to her feet.

She'd been captured.

Her mind went numb for a moment. Time slowed as she tried to make sense of what was happening.

Is this real?

Her worst nightmare had just become a reality, and there was nothing she could do to wake from it.

Jack called her name.

"Go, Jack! Get them out of here!" she yelled. Someone yanked her hair, nearly pulling her off her feet. An arm wrapped around her waist, and she was dragged toward the street.

TWENTY-TWO

Savanah

Walker reached for the doorknob and nodded to Savanah. She raised her bat, ready to charge the men. He yanked open the door and it banged against the wall, causing Savanah to jump. Her heart was racing. Pure adrenaline propelled her through the open door behind Walker. He rushed toward the men. Luckily, the taller of the two had his back to the door. The second man was leaning against a box truck. He straightened and looked their way.

Walker hit the taller man in the back with the full weight of his body. As the two men crashed to the ground, Savanah hauled back her bat and swung, hitting the second man in the shoulder. He swung around to face her, raising a large tactical knife and jabbing it at her. She jumped back a second before it would have made contact with her abdomen. He lunged but tripped on Walker's feet as he and the tall man wrestled for the pistol in the man's hand.

Savanah swung again, this time making contact with the shorter man's head. He dropped to one knee and fell forward, catching himself with his outstretched right arm. As Savanah swung again, she spotted the members of her group from the corner of her eye. They were on the move. Anger and fear pulsed through her veins. She raised the bat over her head and slammed it down on top of the man's skull. He fell forward on his face, unmoving. Savanah kicked him in the ribs as she watched Isabella and the others slip inside the vacant warehouse. Kylie reached out for her. That's when she noticed the duct tape. Her heart broke for her baby girl.

Rushing around the dead man, Savanah moved quickly toward Walker and the tall man. Walker had his hand on the gun, but so did the man. His finger was just outside the trigger guard. She had to stop him before he got off a shot and brought the rest of his crew down on them. Savanah leaned forward and kicked the man in the head with all her might, allowing Walker to roll onto his side. Savanah smacked the attacker repeatedly in the back with the bat, but he refused to release his grip on the pistol.

Walker slammed the man's hand against the pavement of the parking lot, and the gun went skidding away. The man cried out. Savanah drew in a quick breath and held it. She spun around, waiting for the other bad men to arrive, standing with her feet apart, and bat raised. They would have to go through her to get inside that warehouse. Behind her, she heard the muffled cries of the man. She took a chance and glanced back. Walker had both hands tightly gripped around the man's throat; his face was red and his eyes wide with terror, his mouth open as he tried to get air.

Strangling someone took a lot of strength and time. Walker's arms were shaking. How long could he hold on? The sunlight glinted off the barrel of the gun, and Savanah ran to retrieve it. She rushed back, dropped to her knees, and pressed it against the man's temple, all while keeping watch for his compatriots. Had they heard him cry out? Were they planning to attack them? What the hell were they waiting for?

A moment later, the man stopped resisting and went limp. Walker pressed two fingers against the man's neck. "He's dead."

"Let's go," Savanah said.

"Not yet. We need to drag them inside."

"What?" She just wanted to get to her babies. "Why?"

"It will buy us time. If they spot two dead men in the parking lot, they'll know we escaped."

Savanah got to her feet, Walker grabbed one of the first man's arms, and the two of them dragged the dead man into the store. They hauled the second man inside the same way. Walker pulled the door closed, leaving the dead bodies concealed inside. When Savanah turned toward the warehouse, she spotted the pool of blood where the man she'd bashed had fallen.

"Walker." She pointed to the crimson stain.

Walker spun in circles, scanning the back of the store, and then turned toward the warehouse. He ran over and yanked on the rubber mat just outside the warehouse doors. He pulled it over and covered the stain. It wouldn't be immediately visible, but the rug was out of place, though might be enough to buy them time. They needed all the time they could get.

Walker and Savanah ran through the dark warehouse, finally making it out the other side and onto Eighth Street. Walker stopped and scanned up and down the street. "It's clear."

"Do you see the others?" Savanah said.

"No."

That was a good thing. That meant that they'd made it down the street and were heading north toward the community center. They were likely already there waiting for them.

Walker raced across the street and ran close to the buildings. Savanah followed, trying to stay near him. Her head whipped back and forth, checking behind them every few seconds. Walker stopped at an alley between two shops, gripping the pistol they'd taken from the man in both hands. Before checking the alley for bandits, he dropped the pistol's magazine and counted the rounds.

"How many?" Savanah asked.

"Four."

Four was good. They'd done well with less before. Walker was a trained law officer. He could take out an attacker with one shot. She backed up one step as he leaned around the corner.

"It's clear," he said.

They crossed the alley and continued west along Eighth Street. When they reached the intersection, Walker scanned the street to the south and then to the north before stepping around the corner of the three-story bank building. They were heading north on Pine. They had three blocks to go to reach the others.

Savanah's knees buckled as they reached the community center. It was surrounded by marauders. They were laughing and throwing bricks and bottles at the windows. Walker grabbed her by the arm, placed a hand over her mouth, and pushed her behind a florist's van.

"Quiet, Savanah."

She wasn't aware she'd said anything.

"Quiet. It's okay. We'll think of something. They are all outside. They haven't made it in." Walker's eyes darted back and forth between the vehicle behind them and the van in front of them.

"What are we going to do, Walker? My babies," Savanah whispered.

"Let me think."

He leaned down and looked under the van.

"What are you doing?"

"Looking at the fuel tank. It's not punctured."

"What?"

"There might be enough fuel in it."

"It won't start. It's too new."

"I don't need it to start. I just need that fuel to catch fire."

He stood and grabbed her hand.

"You want to create a diversion?" she asked.

"It's the best I've got."

They ran back north along the sidewalk for about thirty feet and stuffed themselves into the entryway of a gift shop. Walker leaned forward and aimed. Just as he was about to squeeze the trigger, Savanah spotted Jane crossing an alley a block over. Behind her were Karson and Keegan. Savanah tapped Walker on the shoulder and pointed.

"They got out," he said.

"We have to get to them and make sure everyone made it out," Savanah said.

Walker ran back to the florist's van and peered around the bumper toward the community center. A second later, he returned to Savanah.

"We need to go back south and find a way to cross the street without being spotted."

"We could lose them." Savanah stared in the direction Jane had traveled.

Walker turned and looked south and then north along Pine Street. He pointed to a pickup truck parked at the curb. "We can try to cross there. We should go at the same time. There would be less of a chance for them to see us."

Savanah nodded. All she wanted was to get to her children. Her mind was racing. She knew they couldn't afford to make careless mistakes. "You're right. We need to be more careful. We'll head back toward Ninth Street and cross where the road bends slightly. I don't think they'll be able to see us there."

It would take time. They'd need to stay low and move slowly to avoid attracting attention. Walker crouched and took off fast-walking, staying close to the cars parked along the curb. They ducked and ran between vehicles. It took at least five minutes for them to make it two blocks. When they reached the intersection, Savanah glanced north toward the community center, trying to determine if they would be seen when they crossed. She couldn't see anyone. The community center building was obscured by the church on the corner of Tenth Street.

"I think we're good." She stepped out onto the street and was about to run across when Walker grabbed her and pulled her back.

"Someone's coming."

She cursed under her breath and edged between a mid-sized sedan and an older SUV. Savanah listened. All she heard was her own labored breathing. "Are you sure?"

He pointed. "Two buildings down on the right side of the street. The ice cream shop. See them. A man and a woman."

Savanah leaned forward and looked where Walker had pointed. She gasped and stood.

"It's Isabella!"

Walker grabbed her arm and pulled her down. "Get down, Savanah. We'll be no good to her if we get ourselves caught."

Savanah yanked away. "The kids. Where's Cayden?" Her mind raced with all the possible dreadful scenarios.

"First things first. We need to get to her. They aren't looking this way. I'm going to cross over and run behind that truck there. You follow me. Stay close. We're going to follow them and wait for a good opportunity to get her back. Then we'll go for the others."

Savanah couldn't think. She was in full panic mode now with the thought of evil men hurting her children. "Okay," she whispered. Isabella would know what had happened to the others. They had to get to her.

"Stay down," Walker whispered as they crept along the street, staying close to the vehicles. They moved from car to car, keeping the vehicles between them and the man with Isabella. Where were they taking her? Would any of their friends be there?

"Maybe we should follow them. He might lead us to the others."

"I don't think so. Why would that crowd still be back at the community center if they'd moved everyone out?"

"You're thinking they caught her as she ran from the building?"

"I am."

Savanah was shaking. She was furious and scared all at the same time. "The others may still be inside? What if they set fire to that building too?"

"First, we get Isabella. She'll be able to tell us what happened and how many of our guys might still be inside."

"How are we going to confront the man without alerting that mob back there?"

"I think you should distract him while I make my way around and surprise him."

"Distract him?"

He pointed. "See that alley there."

She nodded.

"When I reach it, you step onto the sidewalk and call Isabella's name. That will cause them to stop and turn to face you. Keep them talking. I'll go around the building and come at him from behind. Hopefully, I'll get the jump on him, and we can do this quiet like."

"Hopefully?"

"It's the best I've got, Savanah."

She puffed out the breath she was holding and nodded. Walker took off and turned down the alley. The man never turned to look. Walker hadn't been seen. Savanah moved from between the cars and stepped up onto the sidewalk. "Isabella!"

The man spun around, pulling Isabella in front of him like a shield.

"Isabella, are you all right?"

"Yes. The kids are safe," Isabella said before the man punched her in the side of the head.

Isabella bent forward and threw her arms up to block the next blow. The man yanked her back, causing her to trip and almost fall.

He started to turn, but Savanah rushed forward. "Stop. Where are you taking her?"

"Stay right there," the man said. "I'll hurt her. Stay right there."

"I'm not armed. I just want to know where you are taking my friend."

"None of your business," the man spat. He was shorter than Isabella, his hair long and dirty though he wasn't as thin as everyone in Savanah's group. They'd been stealing food from families. They were killers and thieves, and they needed to be stopped.

"What if I want to come too? I don't want to be left out here all alone."

The man's eyes fixed on her. She could feel them perusing her body. She felt naked and exposed. It made her sick.

"Come this way," he said. "Slowly. Let me see your hands."

Savanah took a step forward with her arms bent at the elbows and palms facing out to show him she had nothing in her hands. She took another step, and then another.

Where the hell is Walker? There was no way she was surrendering herself to this lunatic. No way.

Savanah inched forward, trying to buy Walker more time to get into place. She was within ten feet when she spotted movement behind the man but she kept her eyes fixed on him. He was smiling ear to ear, his yellow rotted teeth on full display. The sight of them made Savanah sick to her stomach. The thought of him touching her made her skin crawl. She couldn't imagine how Isabella felt with his arm around her neck.

Walker closed the distance in a flash and pressed the pistol against the back of the man's skull. He whispered something Savanah could just hear over the sound of her pulse beating in her ears. She felt bile rise into her throat and nausea coming on.

Walker hauled the man's head back and slammed the pistol into his skull. He dropped to the ground in a heap. Isabella rushed toward Savanah and threw herself into her arms. Savanah stroked her hair as Isabella sobbed into her chest. "It's all right now. I've got you. You're safe." She took hold of Isabella's shoulders and pushed her back to expose her face. "Isabella, where are my kids? Where are the others? Are they still in the community center?"

"They all got away. I was in the rear, making sure everyone made it out the back. That pervert grabbed me. I told Jack to make sure they kept running."

"Where are they headed?"

"Kurthwood," Isabella said through sobs.

TWENTY-THREE

Will

After some discussion, the group decided to move the Dongfengs back to the intersection a mile or so south of the roadblock. Will drove one of the Chinese military's Humvee-like vehicles to a spot behind a barn near the intersection. He exited the vehicle and readied the 120mm rocket-propelled grenade launcher, reciting to himself Pete's instruction on how to fire the shoulder-launched, anti-tank rocket-propelled weapon. He tried to put the fact that the weapon was made in China out of his mind as he prayed that this one weapon was not a defectively manufactured Chinese product.

Pete and Jason occupied the opposite side of the road with Rob and two others farther down. They'd strike any vehicle that managed to get through. A six-person team, including the lanky kid who'd led them to the IEDs, remained at the roadblock; they were armed with only the PLA soldiers' rifles and a few hand grenades. Will hoped that they wouldn't be needed.

As the convoy came into view, Will faced the intersection and aimed the PF-98 to the left slightly. He steadied himself, not knowing how big a kick the rocket launcher would have. At the same time he fired, Pete and Jason did the same. The convoy stopped. Will had hit the first vehicle. The sound was deafening. A huge ball of smoke arose from the vehicle. Will inserted a second 120mm round into the weapon's breech and fired again. As he did, two soldiers exited and attempted to run for cover. They didn't make it far. Pete or Jason must have fired at them and taken them down.

The third and fourth Dongfengs in the line had been hit, and soldiers were fleeing the armored vehicles. Rob, who was hiding on the opposite side of the road, fired the Chinese-made automatic rifle, mowing down three of the enemy before they could make it to the field beyond the road. A second later, he fired again and took out the three racing through the field.

One enemy soldier almost made it to the old farmhouse one hundred yards from the road. Will heard a shot, and the man dropped. Will reloaded the rocket launcher and shifted south to a point where he could fire upon the last vehicle in the line. It was backing away. The round landed on the hood, but nothing happened. Will ran back and reloaded. By the time he returned, the vehicle had reached the bend in the road. It was just about to disappear when a loud boom sounded to the right of Will. Smoke rose, and men fled. Automatic gunfire stopped their retreat.

One of the teens walked out of the woods, his QBZ-191 Chinese-made assault rifle resting on his shoulder. Pete yelled, but it was too late. One of the soldiers fired his pistol, and the kid fell to one knee. He attempted to raise the rifle and fire, but a second and third round slammed into him, knocking him back. Will felt sick. He was so young. The boy had had his whole life ahead of him. And now it was over. Ended by a foreign invader. Anger boiled in Will's chest. He dropped the grenade launcher and slung his rifle around the front. He raised it and took aim but before he could fire, Pete sprayed the PLA soldiers with automatic gunfire, emptying the magazine into them. After, he walked over and shot each one in the head with his pistol.

He stopped and stood over the body of the kid, made the sign of the cross, and moved back towards Will. The two of them cleared each vehicle. Some of the soldiers had escaped. They were on foot without food or water. They wouldn't last long. They'd likely die of dehydration or run into outlaws. Either way, they were very little threat to the president or his Doomsday plane.

Will and the others collected the weapons and loaded them into two of the Dongfengs. The others were too damaged to move. Eventually, the rest of their comrades would arrive and find the scene. Will was sure they'd send out someone to look for them. They'd want to know if it was a military unit that did this.

"Let's head back to the store and let the others know how we've done. We'll rest up for the night and then head south to engage the enemy tomorrow," Pete said.

Rob drove one of the armored vehicles, and Jason took the other. Will sat in the back of the second Dongfeng staring out the window, his stolen assault rifle resting against his leg. Against all the odds, they'd managed to accomplish what they'd set out to do. They'd stopped the convoys from reaching Shreveport. In addition, they'd confiscated rifles, RPGs, frag grenades, ammunition, pistols, and mortars. Not enough to fight a major battle, but enough to make trouble for the Chinese. As they headed east toward their families, Pete's cousin and his neighbors returned to their homes to pack up. They'd decided it was time to move their families out of the war zone before the fight arrived at their doorsteps.

Will weighed whether it was a good idea to send the rest of their group ahead with them. They weren't all that safe at the store. Not with units breaking through the front lines and racing north. If the soldiers had been able to contact their command, they would have told them of the trouble and the Chinese forces could have decided to swing wide to avoid the roadblocks, which could put them rolling through Roseville right past the store at any time. He'd need to speak to Jason and Pete about it when they got Roseville.

Isabella would protest, Will was sure of that. But Savanah was ready to keep moving. She would do her best to convince the others. Pete might not be too willing to send his family ahead. It would depend on how much he trusted his cousin, Will thought.

Rob slowed the vehicle near the outskirts of town and then pulled into the abandoned car lot. They drove around to the side of the building and parked the Dongfengs there. They didn't want to park them out front for the Chinese or marauders to see. Will was sure that anyone in town would be able to hear the vehicles rolling through and would likely come looking for them. Rob and August agreed to take the first shift, staying with the vehicles and stolen weapons. Will, Pete, and Jason would relieve them in a few hours so everyone would get some rest and time with their families.

They fast-walked six blocks north and turned on Sixth Street. Pete rounded the corner first and stopped. Will, not seeing anything, walked past him. Pete grabbed him and pulled him back to the side of the old pharmacy building.

"What?" Will asked, trying to see for himself.

"Outlaws," Pete said, moving quickly back the way they'd come.

"What? Where?"

"They're at the store," Pete said without stopping.

Jason cursed and rushed ahead of Pete. They turned left on the next block and cut through an alley to make it back to Sixth Street about half a block from the store then stopped and crouched beside a dumpster. Pete was scanning the building through the scope of his rifle.

"How many?" Will asked.

"Shit!" Pete spat. "They're inside the store." He stood and ran back down the alley.

"What are we going to do?" Will's heart was pounding inside his ears as he imagined the worst but tied not to panic. Jason just looked pissed. He gripped his rifle and held it, ready to mow down anyone that got in his way. "Where are we going?" Will asked. Pete didn't answer.

They returned to Fifth Street, turned right, and ran through the intersection. Sprinting to Pine Street, they turned right and ran, crouched low, along the sidewalk, staying close to all the parked and abandoned cars along the curb. Will knew where they were going now. They were heading toward the community center. One of the many places they'd selected as alternate shelters for the group.

Will spotted the men milling about in front of the center, and his heart sank. He fought back despair and panic as they moved between a truck and SUV to avoid being seen by the men. "They're not there," Jason repeated over and over as if trying to convince himself.

Pete pointed. "There. We need to get around and get a look at the back of the center."

He sprinted across the sidewalk and the parking lot between two buildings and disappeared around the back of the building. Jason ran past Will and also disappeared from view. Will was winded and having trouble keeping up. When he reached the back of the building, he saw Pete on the ground wrestling with a man. Jason rushed over toward them, but a second man appeared from nowhere and tackled him.

Now he was struggling to free his rifle from the man's grasp. Will stopped and brought his rifle up to fire but couldn't get a clear shot on either of their attackers. Pulling his knife from its sheath on his belt, Will lunged and jumped on the man's back as Jason rolled him over. The knife slid easily between his ribs but he continued to have a firm grasp on Jason's rifle. Will yanked the knife from the man's body and plunged it in again and again until he released the weapon and rolled off Jason who sprang to his feet and landed on top of Pete's attacker, sending his elbow into the back of the man's neck. He went limp, and Pete managed to pull himself out from under him.

By that time, Jason had already taken off for the community center. Will caught up with him two buildings down. They slid into the recessed entryway and watched as people came and went from the back door. There was no sign of Isabella or the rest of the group.

"Maybe they didn't come here," Will whispered.

"They could be anywhere, Will."

Jason sounded defeated. Will understood the feeling, but he couldn't accept that his family had been captured by the marauders.

"Where would they take them?" Jason asked as Pete caught up with them.

"Their headquarters. Those apartments just off the highway. That's where they're operating out of at the moment."

"Let's go," Jason said, moving back into the alley.

"Stop. We need to search the rest of the town first. They could be anywhere. They could be hiding out in any of these buildings. We can't just go running off and abandon them," Will said.

"Will's right. They could be holed up in one of the buildings near the store. We should check out the warehouse across the alley first and maybe the church on Chestnut Street. Those are both good places. Jack and I checked them out. He might have taken them there."

"Walker would have moved them someplace where they had an easy means of escape. The church is my best guess."

After a thorough search of the warehouse, they reached the church. They weren't there. There wasn't even a sign that they'd been there.

Jason crossed and stopped at the back of the barbershop. He pulled his rifle to his cheek and scanned back toward the community center.

"You aren't going to shoot them?" Will asked. "You'll bring them all down on us."

"I'm looking for someone?"

"Who?"

"Their leader," Jason said, and then he lowered his rifle. "He's not one of them."

"We have to hurry and find our families," Will said, tugging on his arm.

Jason nodded. "When I find him…"

"I know." Will felt the same anger, but they couldn't afford to let rage cloud their judgment.

~

Rob and August were as anxious to find their families as Will, Pete, and Jason. Jason jumped behind the wheel of the Chinese military vehicle and slammed the door. Will crawled in and climbed into the turret. He wasn't even sure how to load the weapon. Pete tapped him on the leg, and he moved into one of the back seats, allowing Pete to man the heavy machine gun.

Will twisted in the seat to see if Rob and August were behind them as Jason sped north. They were and remained right on the bumper as they turned down one street and then another before Jason abruptly pulled the vehicle to a stop in the middle of the road. He quickly exited the vehicle and rummaged in the back, retrieving weapons and ammunition before running around to the front.

Will exited the vehicle and joined the others in the middle of the street. He looked down at what everyone was staring at.

Meet You At The Second Rally Point was scrawled across the pavement in bright pink sidewalk chalk. Savanah was letting them know they'd made it out and where to meet up with them. Tears spilled over Will's eyelids and rolled down his cheeks. He wiped them with the hem of his T-shirt and sprinted back to the Dongfeng. They needed to get to Kurthwood before the scavengers caught up with them—or the Chinese.

TWENTY-FOUR

Savanah

ROSEVILLE, VERNON PARISH, LOUISIANA

Walker, Savanah, and Isabella moved quickly west along Twelfth Street, following the route the group had agreed. When Savanah spotted the words written across the roadway in pink sidewalk chalk, she nearly broke down in tears. "Kylie," Savanah whispered. She'd fought with her about bringing chalk. There was only so much room in her tiny pack, and she needed all the room she could get for clothes and essentials.

"Will and the others will know where to find us," Isabella said.

Walker stared down at the writing. "That was smart thinking."

Savanah looked back, making sure they weren't being followed. They'd need to hurry to catch up with the others who had at least a thirty-minute head start according to Isabella. She hadn't wanted to discuss what had happened between the time the man had captured her and when she and Walker had rescued her. Her focus was on catching up with the group but Savanah knew that eventually, she would need to talk about and process it. She was all too familiar with such trauma. Hopefully, she could help Isabella once they reached the shelter. There may even be counselors there. Lord knew they all could use some therapy after everything they'd been through.

They walked in silence for several miles as Savanah thought about life in Texarkana. She wasn't looking forward to giving up her freedoms to be taken care of by the government, but the alternative was giving up all her freedom and being held prisoner inside a Chinese camp. The two did not even compare.

"How long do you think it will take Will, Jason, and the others to catch up?" Isabella said, breaking the silence.

"Not long," Walker said. "Once they take care of their business, they'll come to Roseville and see Kylie's chalk drawing. They'll move quickly to Kurthwood."

Take care of their business? Their business involved confronting a foreign army. Savanah had tried her best not to think about her brother and Jason fighting against well-armed soldiers. Although she'd disapproved of the plan, she understood their motivation, hating the thought of the country being taken over by the communist regime. Even if they were to restore the electricity and reopen stores and provide food, she didn't want to live under communism. She didn't want that for her children either.

Even before they attacked the nation with the electromagnetic pulse, there'd been a push by some in the country toward socialism. She'd never understood how those for it couldn't see that it was only a gateway towards communism. The system had never worked in any other country it had been tried. It was foolish to her that anyone could believe that Americans would thrive under such a system.

They turned north and made their way along the outskirts of town, at times crossing through residential yards or business parking lots to avoid being seen. Eventually, they reached the Lake Charles Highway and moved as fast as they could in the northbound lanes, though Savanah was disappointed when they reached the highway and didn't see anyone waiting for them there. She understood, and she would have pushed the group on as well. She just needed to know that all her children were safe and together. She marched in front of Walker and Isabella, pushing herself harder and harder to reach them. Sweat poured down her face. Savanah wiped it away on the sleeve of her shirt. She was feeling a little lightheaded. She needed water, but they didn't have time to go searching for it. She pushed on, ignoring all the signs of dehydration.

As they approached an RV park, Walker veered off the highway and strode toward the office.

"Where are you going, Walker?" Savanah asked.

"Wait there. I'm going to see if I can find water."

"You shouldn't go alone," Isabella called after him.

"I'll be careful."

"I have my water filter, Walker. You don't have to take the risk. We can find a water source up ahead," Savanah said. All she had was a small water bottle though. They needed to be able to carry much more water, so they didn't have to keep stopping.

"I think we need something now," he said as he kept going.

She stopped and crossed over a ditch to the cover of some trees along the road, resting against the trunk of a tree as she watched Walker disappear inside the building. He was right. She was so dehydrated that she couldn't go much farther.

Isabella sat cross-legged on the ground with her back against a tree. She leaned her head back and closed her eyes. They were both spent. Savanah realized that they wouldn't have the energy to catch up with the others and that she may not see her children until in the morning. They might have to walk all night to catch up to them. She was surprised that they'd been able to move so quickly with all the children. Her mind started to imagine that they had been captured by the marauders. The thought grew and took on a life of its own to the point she was in a near panic.

"What if the others didn't escape after all?" she asked.

Isabella opened her eyes. "I saw them running away, Savanah. They're safe. They made it out of town."

"But we should have caught up with them by now. They couldn't have moved so quickly with the kids."

"They were trying to get away. How fast would you have moved if you'd been leading the group?"

She considered it. The other parents would have dug deep to find the physical resources to save their children. Isabella was right. They would have moved away from town as quickly as they could, not stopping until they felt it was safe.

"We'll catch up with them soon. They'll stop and let the children rest as soon as they feel safe," Isabella said.

Savanah thought she saw movement near one of the RVs. She shifted and stared in that direction. "Did you see that?" She pointed.

"What?" Isabella twisted and stared off that direction.

"I thought I saw someone over there."

"Maybe it's Walker looking for water," Isabella said, turning back to face her.

"It wasn't Walker. They weren't wearing a cowboy hat."

Isabella got to her feet and crouched behind the tree. "Should we go warn him?"

"I don't know. If we move from here, we could alert people to our presence and cause more trouble for him," Savanah said.

"I wish he'd hurry up."

"Me too. I hate waiting out here feeling exposed."

A few minutes later, Savanah spotted Walker pressed up against the back of the office building. He must have seen the person as well. He waited there for a few more seconds before sprinting to the cover of the trees then disappeared from view for a moment before reemerging next to them.

"We need to go," he said, heading toward the highway.

"Do you think they saw you?" Savanah asked, taking off after him.

"I can't say. If they did, they didn't seem to want trouble any more than I did."

Isabella flanked his other side. "Did you find water?"

He reached in and pulled out a one-liter plastic thermos. "No one had drained the hot water heater yet."

"Really?" Savanah said. "We could have used that water. Too bad there were people back there."

"Yeah. I will probably be kicking myself for not grabbing another container full."

Walker handed the thermos to Isabella, and she unscrewed the lid and took a long drink. "Maybe we'll find another building or house with water nearby then."

"I don't think we should risk it. Not this close to people. For all we know, the marauders could be staying there," Walker said.

They walked for thirty minutes before stopping again. Savanah's legs and her feet were killing her. The water Walker had found had helped immensely, but it was gone now. They would need to find more; that and food. They needed the energy to keep pushing on. This time, they would all go together to have each other's backs. They had to assume that every building was occupied and proceed with stealth.

"What about there?" Isabella nodded toward a small group of homes just off the highway.

Walker stopped in the middle of the highway and looked in that direction. "Might be worth checking out."

Savanah's stomach flip-flopped. They needed food and water, but she had no idea what kind of trouble they might run into by going into homes. They could find people just like themselves or like the takers they'd just encountered back at the store.

"Let's do it," Isabella said. She exited the highway and turned down a side road.

Savanah followed with Walker several feet away, staying near the edge of the road. His pistol was drawn, and he held it in both hands.

Savanah held her bat down at her side. She ran her left hand over the outside of the pocket of her jeans and fingered her pocketknife. She'd practiced with Jason stabbing a man-sized scarecrow, but the thought of actually having to use it turned her stomach. The image of the man she'd bashed with her bat flashed briefly through her mind but she pushed the thought away and focused on the homes ahead.

"Which one?" she asked.

"Let's start with the closest one and work our way through the neighborhood and back to this one on the left," Walker said.

"Maybe we should go around to the back. It might be best not to be seen on the street," Savanah suggested.

Walker shrugged.

"We can do that. If anyone is occupying these homes, though, we'll eventually run into them."

"I hope not." Isabella crossed her arms over her chest. She was as nervous about their plan as Savanah.

Walker led them around to the back of the first house on their right. Savanah peered inside the large kitchen window as they headed toward the door. Walker pulled open the storm door and then stopped. "You ready?" he asked. Savanah swallowed hard and nodded. She wasn't. She wasn't ready at all to see dead bodies or run into people who might harm them. But, ready or not, they were there.

The door eased open, and the stench assaulted her nostrils immediately. She knew instantly that no one was inside. Not living anyway. There was no way anyone would have remained in there with that smell without opening all the windows.

Walker retrieved his handkerchief from his back pocket and buried his face in it. Savanah covered her mouth and nose with the crook of her arm and followed him inside. He stopped in the kitchen and opened a pantry door. There was nothing but empty canning jars inside. The occupants had eaten every bit of food before they died. Isabella opened all the cabinets. They too were devoid of food. Savanah found a Brita filtering water bottle in one of the cupboards and handed it to Isabella then opened the dish-washer and located a plastic water bottle with a small handle. That would give them twenty-four ounces of water. She pumped her fist up and down in the air.

After failing to find even a cracker in the kitchen, the trio moved farther into the house in search of the hot water heater to fill their newfound bottles. If they were able to get enough water for the rest of the trip, the risk they were taking now would be worth it.

They turned down a short, dark hall and past a bedroom where the door was partially cracked. Two bodies were visible on the bed. Savanah rushed past. She didn't want to see them.

Walker opened the small door in the laundry room and stared at the hose attached to the drain valve at the bottom. He knelt and turned the valve. Nothing happened. No water flowed from the tank. Someone had beaten them to it.

"Let's get the hell out of here," Isabella said, making a beeline for the front door.

Savanah wanted to stop her, but she too could no longer take the smell of the rotting corpses. She gasped for air as soon as she stepped outside, wondering if the smell would stay on her clothes and in her hair. She may never get the memory of it out of her mind.

"Next door?" Isabella asked.

Walker said nothing and headed straight for the front door of the next home. He waited for them to catch up before entering. When he eased open the door, Savanah was pleasantly surprised to not smell rotting flesh. It was very dark inside. Heavy blackout curtains hung over the living room windows. Walker bumped into a piece of furniture and cursed.

"You okay?" Savanah asked him.

"Yeah. I just hit my knee on a stool or something."

"Let's open the curtains, so we don't kill ourselves," Isabella said.

Walker flicked on a small flashlight. It wasn't very bright, certainly not enough to illuminate the room, but it shone enough to light their path toward the kitchen.

Opened cans lined the counter. Whoever had eaten the contents hadn't bothered to throw them out. Empty water bottles were strewn everywhere as well. Savanah doubted that they'd find anything edible there.

After a thorough check of the cabinets and pantry, which confirmed her suspicions, they moved to a small utility room where the hot water heater sat. Walker turned the valve, and a small amount of water trickled out. He immediately shut the valve. "Give me your bottles."

Savanah rushed over and dropped down next to him. He placed the opened bottle under the valve and turned it as Savanah grinned from ear to ear at the sound of the water trickling into the bottle. Walker filled it, then Isabella's, and lastly, the one he'd taken from the RV park. They now each had full water bottles. They could make it last until they reached the rally point and could push harder, knowing they had the means to stay hydrated. She would need to fight the urge to down the whole thing. As parched as she felt, she wondered if she would ever drink enough to be well hydrated again.

"Should we just call it good and get back on the highway?" Savanah asked.

"I really could use something to eat," Isabella said. "I have zero energy left."

She'd been through a harrowing experience that morning and had likely spent a great deal of energy fighting with her attacker. As much as Savanah wanted to cut their losses and get going, she had to respect the needs of Walker and Isabella.

Walker took a sip from his water bottle before screwing on the lid. "Let's try a few more houses. We'll move in and out quickly now that we won't be looking for water."

"Okay," Savanah said.

The next two houses were a bust. There wasn't so much as a bread crumb in either one. The fourth house on the block looked like it had been recently occupied. There was a path worn from the driveway to the front door through the overgrown grass. Savanah stopped and looked at the house. The curtains were drawn. There was no way to know if anyone was inside.

"Maybe we should look somewhere else," Savanah said.

"There could be food inside," Isabella said.

Walker was at the door. His hand was on the knob. "We just need a little something."

Savanah felt uneasy as they entered the small brick house. This home had heavy curtains over the window. Walker flicked on his flashlight, and they rushed toward the kitchen. Isabella pulled open a pantry door and gasped.

"Peanut butter and crackers!"

"What? Really?" Savanah said, rushing over. Walker stood behind her, and they all stared into the closet.

"Someone must be staying here," Savanah said, her mouth salivating at the sight of three jars of the protein-rich spread.

Isabella grabbed a box of crackers and then a jar of peanut butter. She thrust them at Savanah and turned for another.

"This doesn't feel right," Savanah said. "This belongs to someone."

"We need it, Savanah," Walker said.

Isabella handed a jar of peanut butter and a box of crackers to Walker. "I need it. I can't go on without it."

She was right. They needed nourishment to get to the rally point and her children. This was about survival. She had to think of her kids.

"The kids are going to freak when they see this," Isabella said gleefully. They would. None of them had tasted anything like it for such a long time.

TWENTY-FIVE

Isabella

JUST NORTH OF LEESVILLE, VERNON PARISH, LOUISIANA

Isabella scooped peanut butter from the jar and spread it on her cracker. She could feel the carbohydrates, proteins, and sugars energizing her body. Endorphins flooded her brain, and she felt hope return. They were going to make it. She was going to get to Cayden, and Will would find them. Somehow, they would all make it to Texarkana. They were strong and resilient. They'd made it through so many things already. She just needed to remain positive and everything would work itself out.

It was difficult to push away the imagery of the man's hands on her body and his breath on her neck. Every time the thoughts came, she wanted to kill the man all over again. She hated that part of survival. She hated all the faces that haunted her sleep now—the faces of the people she'd killed or who had tried to harm them. Would she ever be free from them? She knew she would never be the same person she was before the lights went out. How could she be? She had so much blood on her hands.

As Walker stuffed their haul into his pack, Isabella searched the drawers for a knife. She was hoping for a strong, sharp knife with which to defend herself. She opened the next drawer and was greeted by a whole array of knives. She selected one and felt the edge of the blade. It was sharp enough. She gripped it in her hand and shuddered at the thought of having to use it. From the way things had gone so far, it was almost a certainty that she would. She looked forward to the day when life wasn't a kill-or-be-killed world.

Walker stuffed the jar he held into his pack and reached for Isabella's and then Savanah's jars. Walker slung his pack over his back as Isabella and Savanah followed him toward the door. As they turned to leave, a door shut. Isabella's heart leaped into her throat. "Walker."

He exited the kitchen, gun drawn. Isabella heard him gasp and froze.

Savanah moved back behind Walker who stepped forward and trained his pistol on the end of the hall.

"Stop!" a male voice yelled. "Drop the pack!"

Walker stepped back. He raised the pistol, but before he could fire, a child yelled, "Dad!"

Savanah grabbed Walker's forearm, pushing the weapon towards the floor. "Walker. He's got a kid."

Walker edged back into the kitchen. His pistol was now pointed halfway between the floor and the door.

"We're leaving," Savanah said, holding her hands out, palms facing toward the man. "We were just looking for food. We're going now."

"I can't let you do that. I got a kid to feed. I can't let you take our food," the man said, stepping toward her.

"Don't," Walker said in a low tone. "Step back. Don't make me drop you."

"Walker, he has a kid," Savanah repeated.

"So do you, Savanah," Isabella said, stepping in front of her. "We're leaving, mister. And we're taking the food. We have family we need to get to. You can find more. I'm sure these houses have something."

"They don't. I've looked for days. At least leave us one jar," the man pleaded.

Savanah turned her back to the man. "Walker."

He huffed, then nodded to the pack on his back. "Just one," he said as she unzipped the pack.

Isabella knew that the presence of the man's child had played on Savanah's motherly heartstrings. Although they desperately needed that food, Isabella understood. Savanah had been one of the few people that had somehow maintained her humanity through this mess. She also knew that it wouldn't be long before the harsh realities of the times crushed every ounce of it from all of them, even Cayden, Kendra, and Karson.

Cayden had witnessed horrendous things already, and she'd seen him change before her eyes. He'd gone from a sweet, kind, thirteen-year-old boy to a tough young man willing to do whatever it took to save his family. No matter how hard Savanah might try, she wouldn't be able to shield her children from the depravity that people had devolved into. It seemed that only two types of people had survived so far—the heartless and the brave.

Savanah approached the man slowly and held out the jar of peanut butter. "I'm sorry. We were looking for unoccupied houses. I hope you and your boy make it."

The man eyed Walker for a moment before reaching out and taking the jar from Savanah. He placed it behind him and backed away. "Rusty, go into the bedroom."

"Daddy. No. They gave you the peanut butter."

Time moved in slow motion as the man's intention dawned on Savanah. Walker pushed her aside and rushed into the living room and Isabella grabbed Savanah and pulled her behind the wall that separated it from the kitchen. Her eyes fixated on the man and her heart sank as he drew the gun from the back of his waistband and raised it. Walker squeezed the trigger of his pistol, and the man fell to the floor. The boy rushed to his side, sobbing into his chest. "Daddy! Daddy!"

Walker grabbed the kid, who looked to be no more than eight or nine. He was so very thin. They certainly hadn't eaten much lately. Isabella's heart broke for them both. She couldn't imagine the man's desperation. It would be torture to see your child waste away like that.

"It's okay, Rusty. I'm okay. It hit me in the vest. It just stings a little." The man lifted his shirt to reveal body armor.

Walker kicked the man's weapon away and aimed his at the man's head. "Don't you move another muscle, or I'll put one right between your eyes."

Isabella grabbed the boy around his waist and lifted him off his feet. He kicked and screamed for his father but she didn't want the kid to see it if Walker had to follow through on his threat. The man had already proven himself stupid.

"Savanah. You and Isabella take my pack and go. I'll catch up with you in a moment," Walker said.

Savanah's mouth dropped open. "There's no need for that, Walker. Just take his pistol. He's not going to try anything else." Her gaze fell on the man. "Right? Tell him."

"I'm done. Just take the damn peanut butter and go. Me and my boy will just stay here and starve to death."

Isabella's anger boiled in her gut. She stepped toward the man as the kid continued to struggle within her grasp. "You really are one stupid MFer, aren't you? It is truly a wonder that you have made it this far without someone putting a bullet in that thick skull of yours. All you had to do was keep that big trap of yours shut and let us leave. Instead, you try stupid shit and then whine like a little bitch. Are we supposed to feel sorry for you? I don't. I feel sorry for this kid, having to rely on you for his survival."

The man's eyes narrowed on her.

"Maybe we should just take the kid and leave you here."

"Isabella, you're scaring the boy," Savanah said as she rushed to her side.

She took the kid from Isabella and placed him down beside his father. "I'm sorry. We're going now. Please don't do anything stupid. I don't want my friends to hurt you or your son."

He glared at Savanah and then Isabella. He really was that stupid.

"Just go. I hope the gangs catch up with you, and then you'll get what's coming to you."

Isabella rushed over to the man and stood over him. Walker took a step closer as well. "What did you say? Are you one of them?" she asked.

He looked away. He was. He was one of the marauders. What were he and his son doing out here all by themselves?

"Why did you leave?" Savanah asked.

"Steve. He's the leader. He didn't much care for kids and didn't want to waste food on anyone that wasn't contributing. He made it almost impossible for me to care for him properly like."

"We're going back for momma as soon as we find some more weapons and ammo," the boy said.

"You left your wife there?" Isabella asked.

He sat up, and Walker kicked him in the breastplate. "Stay down."

"I had to get my boy out. He was starving to death. His mother wanted me to get him away from there. I couldn't get to her." He cleared his throat before continuing. "You can judge me all you want, but I did what I had to for my kid, and I ain't sorry for that."

"We need to go," Walker said. "If they come looking..."

If they came looking for Isabella, Savanah, and Walker, they'd be putting the boy in danger. Savanah rushed to the door and opened it. She peered through the crack. "It looks clear."

"Get up and go into the bedroom. Stay inside. You come out, and I'll drop you," Walker said as he backed toward the door. "Isabella."

"I have your back," she said, holding her knife out in front of her.

"You follow Savanah. I'll watch this asshat until you get to the corner."

Savanah turned and stepped back inside. "No. You come with us. I'm not going without you."

Walker huffed and then stopped at the door. "Okay. Let's just go."

"Wait," the man called after them. "Wait. Are there more of you?"

Walker stopped. "That's none of your business."

"You can take him." The man picked up his son and held him out to Walker. "You can take him with you, and I can go back for his mother." Isabella stared at the man. His eyes were pleading this time. Gone was the contempt she'd seen before. Maybe he really did love his child. It was a self-sacrificing thing to do.

"We can't. We need to..."

"We'll take him," Savanah said, rushing past Walker. "We'll take him for now, and you can meet up with us in Texarkana."

"You're heading to the shelter?" the man asked.

Isabella's gut clenched. Savanah should never have told him that.

"You go get your wife and meet us there." Savanah held her arms out to receive the boy who began to cry uncontrollably. He held tight to his father's neck as he tried to hand him to Savanah.

"Look here, Rusty. I have to go rescue your mom. I can't do that with you tagging along. I can't keep you safe and go back for her." The kid's cries became more of a whimper as he listened to his father. "You want your mom back, right?" The kid bobbed his head up and down. "Go with these people. We will come for you. We'll meet you at the shelter."

"But, Daddy..."

"They have ice cream at the shelter," the man lied.

"They do?"

"They do. You like ice cream. You go with this nice lady and save your mom and me a chocolate cone, okay?"

The child's gaze turned to Savanah. He still wore a questioning look.

"Okay, Pappa."

Savanah took the boy from his father and turned toward the door. "When you and your wife get there, ask for Savanah Fontenot. I will make sure your son gets there. I promise."

Isabella knew that Savanah meant well, but she couldn't promise that any of them would make it to Texarkana. It was highly likely that this boy would never see his parents again. So many children had become orphans during this crisis. He'd likely join their ranks at the shelter, or Savanah would adopt him as her own. The latter was a more likely scenario.

Isabella thought about Will and Cayden. It had been unspoken between them that Isabella would care for Cayden if he didn't return; a thought she couldn't bear. Not that she didn't want to care for Cayden, but the thought of losing Will was more than she could fathom.

"Let's go, Savanah," Walker said, holding open the door.

"I'll see you at the shelter, little man," the father said.

The boy looked back over his shoulder and waved as Savanah placed him down on the ground outside the door.

Isabella said a prayer for Will and started walking back toward the highway.

TWENTY-SIX

Isabella

LANDRY'S AUTOMOTIVE REPAIR, VERNON PARISH,
LOUISIANA

After walking for hours, Walker finally allowed Isabella, Savanah, and Rusty to stop for the day and left the roadway near a long-abandoned automotive garage. Vines covered the bay doors of Landry's Automotive Repair. Walker went around to the side of the building and a second later, Isabella heard a tinkling sound as Walker cleared broken glass from a windowsill. He disappeared inside and reappeared at the small door to the office.

They entered the musty-smelling place without a word, Savanah and Rusty making their way to a far corner to sit on the floor while Isabella pulled up a well-worn office chair and parked herself by the dust-covered window. Walker left to explore the rest of the small building.

Isabella leaned her head back and stared out as the sun slipped over the horizon, her eyelids growing heavy. She longed for a bed with nice, freshly laundered sheets.

"I'll take the first watch," Walker said. "Isabella, you want to take the second shift?"

"Sure."

"Four-hour shifts?" Savanah asked.

"We should do two hours. There are three of us. I'm not sure any of us can stay awake for four," Walker said.

Isabella was asleep almost immediately. Two hours felt like two minutes when Walker woke her for her shift. He handed her the pistol and took a position on the floor on the opposite side of the metal desk. Isabella stood and paced, trying to wake up and stay alert. She moved from the window in the office to the window where Walker had broken into the shop. She could still smell the dirty grease, although it was unlikely that the place had been used in over a decade.

She moved to a small window in a bathroom just off the office. Walker had used a dirty shop towel to wipe the grime off the glass in one spot but Isabella had to stand on her toes to look through it.

She picked up the towel from the floor and began wiping the rest of the pane, staring out over the back alley behind the shop as she did. Behind it was a small house and barn illuminated by the three-quarter moon shining down from a clear sky. Both looked to have been abandoned around the same time as the shop. The front door was open and half off its hinges. Windows were broken out. She was about to turn when she thought she saw movement. She dropped the rag and gripped the pistol in both hands as she stared at the space between the house and barn. She moved to the back door and opened it just a crack.

"Go wake Savanah."

Walker's voice startled her, and she jumped and spun.

"We need to go," he said.

"Did you see someone too?" Isabella asked.

"They're out front as well."

"Oh shit!"

"We're going to try to slip away before they know we're here."

"You think they don't know?"

"Maybe not," Walker said.

Isabella handed him the pistol and moved toward the office. A shadow passed the side window where Walker had entered, and

Isabella jumped back, pressing herself flat against the back wall of the shop. Walker spun around, pointing the weapon in that direction.

"Walker," Isabella whispered. "They're everywhere."

"Hurry. Go wake Savanah. Make sure the kid doesn't make any noise though."

Isabella crouched and ran to the office. Before nudging Savanah, Isabella placed her hand over the kid's mouth. He didn't even stir. He must have been exhausted.

"Savanah," she whispered. "Wake up. We have company."

Savanah bolted upright. "What? How many?"

"I don't know. Several. Walker said to get you and make sure the kid stays quiet. We're going to try to slip out the back."

"And go where? There's nothing but open fields beyond here."

"They can't see us in the dark. We have to go."

Savanah lifted the boy. There was no way she could carry a nine-year-old very far. He needed to walk and keep up with them. She strained to get up with the extra sixty or seventy pounds.

"Let me," Isabella said, helping her to her feet. "You have to let him walk."

As they moved past the window, the boy's eyes opened. "Where are we going?"

"Shhh," Savanah said. "There are bad people outside. We have to get away. I need you to be very quiet." She lowered him to the floor and took his hand. "Can you do that for me?"

He nodded. Even in the dim moonlight coming from the window, Isabella could see the tears welling in his eyes. "Yes," he whined.

"It's going to be okay, son. We're just going to sneak out the back and find another place to sleep, okay?"

"Okay." His voice was timid and shaky. There was no telling what kind of violence the boy had already witnessed in his short life. He had reason to be leery now. Isabella led them back through the shop. As she did, she kept her eyes on the window. As they neared Walker and the back door, Isabella saw a man carrying a rifle. For some reason, she wondered if it could be Will or Pete. They had rifles. She hadn't seen anyone else carrying one for a long time. No one had ammo anymore. They'd been fortunate that Pete had been collecting and hoarding ammunition for years before the EMP, or they'd be in the same boat.

"Walker," Isabella said, bumping his shoulder. "They have rifles."

Isabella knew they need to go, but she didn't want to be shot in the back running from the building.

Walker moved toward the window.

"Where are you going?" Savanah said. "We need to go."

"They aren't the scavengers," Walker said. He grabbed the kid and quickly moved to the door. "That's the Chinese."

TWENTY-SEVEN

Will

Jason sped north along the route that Savanah would have led the group getting out of town. They were on foot and had small children with them. It shouldn't be long before Will and the other guys caught up with them. Will tried to work out how they could quickly get everyone to Kurthwood so he and the others could get back to fighting the Chinese. They had to make sure this time that their families were somewhere safely away from the gangsters and the enemy forces. That might take more time than they had.

Jason was pushing the Dongfeng harder than it was capable of going, speeding through the intersections and past stop signs. They passed a road sign, and Will's heart nearly jumped out of his chest. "Stop!" he yelled. "Stop. We can't go this way."

Jason slowed.

"Fort Polk." Will pointed to the road sign. They were in a Chinese vehicle nearing an army base.

He'd no more than spoken the words before the vehicle Rob was driving exploded. It veered off the roadway and came to a stop in the ditch.

Jason floored the Dongfeng.

"We have to help them."

"We can't help them, Will. They're gone," Pete said.

A moment later, a Joint Light Tactical Vehicle (JLTV) came into view. Jason stopped the Dongfeng as fast as was possible, which was about three seconds slower than necessary. The JLTV's turret turned, and Pete yelled, "Back up! Back up!

"We need to get the hell out of this vehicle, Pete," Jason yelled back. He opened the door and dove out. Will followed on the opposite side and hit the pavement hard, landing on his elbow and right knee. He rolled and stopped short of the ditch. Will jumped to his feet, wanting to put as much distance between him and the Dongfeng as possible. He did not want to be anywhere near the target of the JLTV.

He jumped the ditch and crossed an open field. The sun had nearly set, making it difficult to see the ruts in the dirt. Will's ankle curled, and he went down. Before he could get back to his feet, the Dongfeng exploded. He spun around, looking for Pete and Jason, spotting Jason running through a field on the west side of the roadway. Will scanned back and forth, looking for Pete. He couldn't see any sign of him.

A minute later, several JLTVs approached the burning Dongfeng. The doors opened, and soldiers stepped out, rifles at the ready. Will pressed himself tight to the ground, not wanting to be seen and mistaken for an enemy.

"Let me see your hands! Let me see your hands!" one of the soldiers yelled.

Will raised his head just enough to see if they'd spotted Jason. It looked as if they were pointing their rifles toward the ditch, not the field. They must have found Pete.

"I'm American! I'm on your side," Pete yelled back. Light from the Humvee flooded the area. Will raised himself up on his elbows to get a better look.

"My friends and I fought some Chinese and took these vehicles from them," Pete said.

"Where are your friends?" one of the soldiers said, still standing looking down into the ditch with his rifle trained on Pete.

"They ran when we saw you. We knew you'd fire on the vehicles."

"Reynolds, take Echo Team and track them down."

Will waited, watching to see what the soldiers intended to do with Pete. He wasn't about to give away his position if the soldier was going to shoot them. He wouldn't blame them; the story sounded sketchy even to him.

"Get him up," the soldier standing over Pete said. Two more soldiers dropped down into the ditch and hauled Pete to his feet. A light was shone in his face, and he raised his arm to shield his eyes. The soldiers yanked his hands down and around behind his back.

"Where did you come from?"

"My cousin and some of his neighbors helped my team ambush two convoys of Chinese soldiers over on Highway One Eleven. We learned from an injured Chinese soldier that they were headed to Shreveport. We decided to try to stop them. It's about time we send those MFers back to China," Pete said.

"You were with that bunch that struck the convoys? What the hell are you doing here?"

"Our families are on foot, heading to Texarkana. The place they were staying at while we were away was hit by raiders. They had to flee. We're looking for them."

"Is that a large group with a bunch of women and kids?"

"Yes, have you seen them?"

"They caught a transport truck heading that way. Our colonel has a soft spot for kids."

A surge of joy rushed through Will. They were safe and likely already in Texarkana by now.

"That is awesome news. My friends are going to be thrilled to learn about it." Pete's head swiveled searching for Will. "You hear that, Will. Your family is on their way to Texarkana in military transport."

Will stood and slowly walked toward Pete and the soldiers with his hands in the air.

"That's amazing news," Will said. "You can't get better news than that." They wouldn't have to walk with the kids, and they wouldn't be at the mercy of marauders and outlaws. He was anxious to get there himself now.

"Jason," Will yelled. "Did you hear? Savanah and the others are on military transport."

Jason didn't answer.

Will yelled again as he approached Pete. "Jason, it's okay to come out."

A round whizzed past Will and struck the burning vehicle. It was followed by a barrage of automatic gunfire. Was Jason firing at them?

Will dove into the ditch as the US Soldiers ran for cover and began returning fire. "Is that Jason?" Pete asked.

"I don't think so," Will replied.

The firefight lasted less than five minutes. The firing just stopped, and then the soldiers fanned out in search of the shooters, leaving Will and Pete standing in the ditch wondering what had happened to Jason.

Long minutes passed as the soldiers searched the field for enemy combatants. They returned with two injured Chinese soldiers who were taken to a truck and whisked off, no doubt to be questioned by professional interrogators.

"Sir," Will said.

"Don't call me sir," the soldier said. "I'm Sergeant Hadley."

"Sergeant Hadley," Will said. "Did you see a white guy out there?"

"Private Young, bring that civilian over here."

Jason was bleeding from the back of his head. He looked dazed as the soldier led him across the field. Will and Pete rushed to him, and each took an arm. "We got him," Will said. "You okay, Jason?"

"The damn communist snuck up on me and conked me on the back of the head."

"Did they tell you?" Pete said.

"Tell me what?"

"That Savanah and the others were on a military transport heading for Texarkana. Hell, they may have even arrived there by now." Pete wore an ear-to-ear grin.

Jason's head tilted up, and he looked from Pete to Will. "Is that true?"

"That's what the soldier said," Will replied.

"Oh, thank God!"

Will and Pete lowered Jason to the ground on the opposite side of the road from the burning Dongfeng. They were on foot now and had to decide what they were they were going to do. Back to Merryville to cause the Chinese more trouble or make their way north to Texarkana to be reunited with the families.

"Sergeant Hadley," Will asked. "Did we do any good slowing down the convoy?" Will pointed to the Dongfeng.

Hadley smiled. "You gave us time to move in reinforcements to wipe out the rest of the units that had broken through our lines."

"They won't be making it to Shreveport then?"

"Not today. We've pushed them back across the Intercoastal." Hadley turned to go.

"Can I ask you about the president's plane?" Will asked. He knew the odds of getting such information from the soldier were next to zero, but he was dying to know about the Doomsday plane.

Hadley spun back around. "What? Where did you hear about that?"

"One of the enemy soldiers mentioned the airbase in Shreveport and the Doomsday plane."

"He said Doomsday?" Hadley asked. He gestured for Will to stay put and walked back toward his Humvee. As he did, he spoke into his radio. "Tell Stephens and Lieutenant Sharp I have someone they're going to want to talk to."

Will was more than surprised to be sitting across a table from Analyst Rachel Stephens and Lieutenant Ryan Sharp from back in Houston. Stephens looked much better than the last time he'd seen her. The gash above her eye from when the air museum blew up on top of her had healed but had left a scar.

"So, how did you come across this injured Chinese soldier?"

Will told her the story leading up to him finding the injured soldier and asking the kid why they were in such a hurry to get to Shreveport.

"And he specifically mentioned the president?" Sharp asked.

"No. He mentioned the airbase and then Doomsday. It was Pete that said that the airfield there was where the presidential Doomsday plane might land. I put two and two together." He smiled. "Was I right? Did the president survive this mess? Is he in Shreveport?"

Stephens slowly pushed her chair back and stood. "That's classified."

TWENTY-EIGHT

Will

FORT POLK, VERNON PARISH, LOUISIANA

Stephens left the room for a moment and then returned. She sat back down, but this time all she wanted to know was how Isabella and Cayden were doing.

"I'm so sorry about Betley. I know that Isabella took it hard."

They'd only known FBI Agent Betley for a few days when he'd been killed in the insurgents' attack on Ellington Field Joint Reserve Base. Isabella had taken it hard. She also took it hard when the Chinese spy, Kim Yang, had been killed. She was a very compassionate person. Unfortunately, she'd seen so much death since then that it hardly fazed her anymore. They'd all been hardened by the violence they'd witnessed.

"I appreciate that, Stephens. I'd ask what you've been up to, but I know how you'd reply."

Surprisingly, she began describing her trip to Fort Hood and subsequent trip to Fort Polk. Will had been so stoked about the military assets that had been sent to secure the command center at Texarkana that he barely heard her when she mentioned the recruiting mission the military was undertaking.

"We are so close right now, Will. So very close to winning and pushing the Chinese out of Texas, Louisiana, and Mississippi. It's been citizens like yourself stepping up to defend their homeland that has made the difference. I heard what you and your crew did to stop the Chinese from reaching Shreveport. That was very brave." She tucked a stray strand of her brown hair back into its bun and smiled.

"We couldn't just let them take over the country without a fight. Unfortunately, Isabella and the rest of our group came under attack by bandits while we were fighting the Chinese. They were forced to flee, but the good news is that they were picked up by the military and—"

The door flew open, and a soldier rushed in. He saluted Lieutenant Sharp and handed him a piece of paper. He glanced over at Stephens. "I have to go."

"Trouble?" Stephens asked.

His gaze switched to Will and then back to Stephens. "Alpha team just spotted an enemy unit about ten miles north of Roseville. They are engaged with some civilians. One of the civilians claims to be a Texas Ranger."

"Texas Ranger?" Will's heart sank. It couldn't be. They were on their way to Texarkana.

"What is this Ranger's name?"

Despite Sharp's admonishment to stay put at the base, Will was determined to go. He needed a vehicle. But taking one of the military's Humvees would likely get him shot. He found Pete and Jason eating MREs near the front gate of the post. They had to find a way to get to their families, come hell or high water. He had to get to them before they got caught in the middle of this damn war.

Pete jumped to his feet. "Hadley owes us." He took off in search of Hadley though Will thought it was a waste of time. Hadley wasn't going to let them tag along even if they had stopped a Chinese convoy heading for Shreveport. What they needed to be doing was scouring the area outside the base for a running vehicle.

"Wait up," Jason yelled after Pete. Will threw up his hands in frustration and took off after the two men.

"Absolutely not," Hadley said after they caught up with him preparing to leave.

"It's our families. We have to go," Pete said.

"But I don't have to take you. I'm not getting my ass handed to me for breaking regs. You should stay put here and let us handle this."

Pete stepped closer to the sergeant. "Our families are in danger right now because we chose to fight for our country. All we're asking for is a ride. We aren't asking you to give us weapons or anything."

Hadley turned his back on Pete. He pointed to a military truck. "It's a piece of shit. We borrowed parts from every vehicle on the base to keep it running, and it still runs like crap."

Pete sprinted toward the truck with Jason and Will close behind him.

"I'm going to say you stole it if anyone notices it missing," Hadley called.

"Whatever," Pete said as he yanked open the door and climbed into the driver's seat.

Pete pulled in line with the other military vehicles. Will had been shocked when somehow, by a miracle perhaps, they made it there. Pete stopped the truck in the middle of the road, threw open the door, and ran. Will, too jumped out and ran toward the fighting. Jason passed him. Will struggled to keep up. He was huffing and puffing as he dropped down beside Jason and Pete as they crouched behind one of the Humvees.

Hadley came up behind them. "I'm surprised you three made it. I was sure that old truck would leave you stranded on the road."

Pete ignored him. "Where're our families?" Pete asked.

"As far as I know, it's just two women. The Ranger said they got separated from their group. They were on their way to meet up with them when they got surrounded by enemy combatants."

Will's heart sped up. He'd guessed it was Savanah and Isabella inside that building. They'd be the ones that would have made sure that the others made it safely away, putting themselves in danger. Savanah would have made sure her kids had an opportunity to escape the marauders back there at Roseville.

"The Ranger said they tried to make a run for it out a back door, but a barrage of bullets sent the ladies back inside. He was too far away to make it and had to dodge bullets to escape. Soldiers patrolling the area heard the firefight and found the Ranger up on the roof of a nearby building firing down on a team of Chinese soldiers. He had them pinned down while the rest of their unit fired upon the building where the ladies are."

"They're still inside?" Will asked.

"Yeah, but now the Chinese are firing at my guys. We should have them eliminated shortly. Why don't you three go back to the truck and wait for us to take care of these ass wipes? We have things under control here."

Will didn't believe him. It sounded more like they were in a heavy firefight, and the Chinese were in control. Will was afraid that they might use mortars to take out the building where Isabella and his sister were holed up.

"We need weapons, Hadley. You need us, man. Look at this mess. They are eating your lunch," Pete said, pointing to the burning vehicles.

As soon as the words left his mouth, an explosion rocked one of the JLTVs. The gunner turned in the turret and began firing very close to the building. Isabella and Savanah were going to get caught in the crossfire. He had to do something.

"Jason, we have to get them out of there."

Pete stood in a crouch and took off around a clump of bushes. "Follow me."

Will did, but Hadley grabbed hold of Jason. That was the wrong thing to do. Jason hauled back and landed a hard blow to the side of the man's head. As he went down, Jason, Will, and Pete took off toward the building.

Pete dropped to the ground behind an old beat-up wrecker. Two of its tires were missing, and the hood was up. Bullets bounced off the hood, causing sparks to fly. Will wasn't sure what Pete had planned but hoped it involved getting some kind of weapons of their own because so far, this was looking like a suicide mission. Pete pulled his tactical knife and pointed to three Chinese soldiers pinned down by the JLTV's machine guns about one hundred feet to their right. "I'll be back," he said. He took off in a crouch, running in a zigzag pattern as rounds whizzed over his head. "

"What in the hell is he doing? Is he crazy?" Jason said.

"I think so."

Crazy or stupid, Will thought.

Pete pounced on the soldier in the back, and in seconds, he turned the man's rifle on his comrades. They went down, and Pete grabbed their rifles. He turned toward Will and Jason and waved for them to join him. Will and Jason stared at one another for a second before Will stood in a crouch. He took off running first, but Jason beat him to where Pete was gathering up ammunition for the rifles. Will was so winded by the time he reached Pete that he was lightheaded and breathing heavily. He felt so useless. Malnourishment had rendered him totally ineffective. How was he going to help anyone when he couldn't even run fifty feet?

Pete shoved a rifle into his chest and then three spare magazines. "Put these in your back pockets," he said. Jason was trying to find the button to drop the magazine on the Chinese-made weapon. Pete took it from him and depressed the button before dropping the magazine. He slammed a new one back in, pulled the charging handle, and then handed it back to Jason. "Watch yourself. They appear to jam a lot."

Will pulled the stock to his shoulder and looked through the scope. The night vision illuminated several more groups of enemy fighters between them and the building. They seemed to be pretty well concealed from the US Soldiers along the front of the building. Will scanned to his left. A team of soldiers was slowly making their way around to attack them from the rear. He watched a second longer before Pete tapped him on the shoulder. "Let's move out."

His stomach flip-flopped as he prayed he could find the strength to do what he needed to do. He sucked in a deep breath and let it out before falling in behind Jason. He ran with the rifle trained on the backs of the enemy and waited until Pete began firing to pull the trigger of his rifle. The rifle jammed! He pulled the charging handle as he ran, trying to remove the round in the chamber. It went flying out, and another one was chambered as he let go of the handle. He fired, and the round discharged. He couldn't say if he hit anything.

Pete ran to the back of a pickup truck and dropped down to a crouch. He was firing over the hood when Will reached him. Jason was near the truck's bed, firing at the same group of enemy soldiers. They turned their attention away from the US Soldiers advancing on them to return fire upon Pete.

Rounds peppered the truck, shattering all the glass that remained in the old pickup. Pete dropped down by the tire and switched out the magazine for a fresh one. Jason moved forward into Pete's position and began shooting. Will placed the barrel of the rifle on the bed of the truck, looked through the scope, and found a target. He squeezed, and the soldier slumped forward. He found a second target just as rounds struck the opposite side of the truck. He ducked and waited for the fusillade to stop before returning fire.

The enemy soldiers pivoted to face the front of the building where Isabella and Savanah were hiding. Will scanned that direction. US Soldiers were nearing the door. They were out in the open. The Chinese fired, and one after another went down. US Soldiers were taking fire from two sides. Will couldn't see the enemy that was firing from the opposite side of the building.

Will didn't know why the Chinese were interested in either the building or his family. All he knew was that he had to do something to get to them. He took the opportunity to move up behind the enemy soldiers. Will squeezed the trigger, and the rifle fired on full auto. He sprayed the combatants as he ran towards them. Two went down. A third turned toward him. Pete ran past Will just as he fired. The round struck Pete, and he went down. Will returned fire, and the combatant dropped to the ground. The two other Chinese soldiers continued firing upon the army soldiers at the front of the building.

"Get to the back door, Will. I've got these two," Jason said, hopping over one of the dead men. Will didn't look back as he sprinted toward the building. He expected to be mowed down, but somehow, Jason must have distracted them or taken them out. Will's already injured shoulder hit the back wall of the building hard, and pain shot through him. He fought back a wave of nausea and pressed himself against the building, wasting no time reaching for the door. He yanked on the doorknob, but it was locked.

"Isabella! Savanah!" he yelled.

Gunfire sprayed the windows of the building, forcing him to dive to the ground. He rolled then got to one knee. He couldn't see where the rounds were coming from. He looked through the scope and scanned to his right slightly. Jason was in a wrestling match over his rifle. The combatant had both hands on the weapon and

Jason was shaking him around like a rag doll, but he couldn't seem to shake the man off. Will fired, and the man released his grip. Jason turned the weapon around and struck him in the face with the stock of the rifle. The man fell straight back and didn't get back up.

A round whizzed by Will and struck the door to the building. While Jason began firing in the direction from which it had come, the door flew open, and Savanah screamed.

TWENTY-NINE

Savanah

LANDRY'S AUTOMOTIVE REPAIR, VERNON PARISH, LOUISIANA

"Will!" Savanah called out.

"Was that Will?" Isabella asked as the two women rushed toward the back door and the sound of the male voice calling their names.

As they reached the back, bullets tore through the window, sending glass flying into the room. Savanah dove, slamming her knee on the concrete floor and sliding across the small room. Isabella screamed, and rounds continued to strike the building.

"Will!" Savanah yelled. They were shooting at her brother. She had to get to him. She crawled over to the door, grabbed the doorknob, and pulled herself up. When she yanked open the door, the first thing she saw was Jason, covered in blood with an enemy soldier standing behind him with his arm wrapped around Jason's neck.

"Jason!"

A shot rang out, and the soldier released his grip on Jason. As he slumped to the ground, Savanah took off running toward them. "Jason! Are you hurt?"

"Savanah, get down!" Jason yelled. He ran toward her with one arm outstretched. Just before he reached her, a bullet struck him.

He stopped, pivoted, and brought the rifle up. Savanah was knocked to the ground. Will was on top of her.

"Stay down, Savanah. Stay down."

"Jason!" Savanah continued to call his name. Instead of responding to her, he dropped to one knee, his left arm dangling at his side. He lifted the rifle with his right arm and began firing. With Will shielding her body, Savanah couldn't see where the shooter was but did know they were out in the open and exposed. They needed to get back inside the building.

"Help him, Will," Savanah cried.

"I have to get you back inside," Will said, yanking her to her feet by her arm.

"No, we have to get Jason."

Will pulled her backward as Jason continued shooting.

"Jason!"

"Get inside, Savanah!" Jason yelled.

Isabella grabbed Savanah's other arm and tugged on her. "I got her, Will. Help Jason," she said.

"We have to go, Savanah. We're unarmed. This place is swarming with fighters."

Savanah looked back as Isabella pulled her toward the building. Soldiers were advancing toward Will and Jason. She couldn't tell whether they were Chinese or American. "Will, behind you."

He turned. "Don't point that thing in this direction," a soldier called in English.

Relief washed over Savanah. They were friendlies. They'd come to save them. Will and Jason would survive, and she would see her children again. The joy of the moment was overwhelming.

"Isabella, the Army is here." Tears streamed down her cheeks.

Isabella stopped and turned to see them for herself. She let go of Savanah's arm and placed her hand over her mouth. Both women were crying as the army raced past Will and Jason to engage the enemy. Will rushed to Jason and helped him to his feet, and they ran back toward the building. Savanah grabbed Jason and wrapped both arms around his neck. "Please tell me you're okay."

"I'm fine. It's just a small wound," Jason said.

"Let's get pressure on it and stop the bleeding," Will said, placing a hand on the small of Isabella's back and leading her inside.

～

Will found a first aid kit in the office of the garage, wrapped Jason's arm tight, and made a sling out of old shop towels. The gunfire outside had stopped by the time he'd finished, and a US Soldier appeared at the back door. "Nice shooting, Blanchard. How's the arm?"

"I'll live. Did you see Pete?"

The soldier nodded. He's with the medics. I think he'll make it."

"Thanks, Hadley," Jason said, wrapping his good arm around Savanah's shoulders. Thanks for getting there when you did."

"I told you to wait in the truck. Now I'll have to spend half a day writing a report on why civilians were running around with Chinese rifles," Hadley said. "Not to mention how you stole that old deuce and a half."

"Speaking of that," Jason said. "We could really use that to get to Texarkana."

"I can't let you do that."

"Man, we need to get to our kids," Jason said.

"I can't give you an army vehicle." Hadley looked to the soldier beside him. "But I might get you a ride with the next unit going that way."

Jason smiled. "We would greatly appreciate it."

Hadley nodded.

"You okay, guys?" Walker's face appeared in the space that had once been a window.

"We're fine," Will said.

"It's damn good to see you guys," Walker said.

"You should let the medic take a look at that arm before you head to Texarkana." Hadley and the other soldier turned to step outside.

"I'll do that," Jason said. "And thanks again, Hadley."

While they waited for a vehicle to transport them to Texarkana, Will, Jason, and a recovering Pete, filled them in on their success repelling the Chinese convoy that had been heading for Shreveport. Savanah was deep in thought about the news of a possible Doomsday plane landing in there with the president and maybe even members of his cabinet. The implications being that there was hope that life could return to something akin to normal someday soon. Why else would he be in the area when there were enemy combatants so close?

"The medic said they had docs and medical equipment at Texarkana. They've set up a field hospital there for wounded soldiers. They even have electricity, if you can believe that," Pete said, a smile spreading across his face.

"Electricity?" Isabella asked. "Is that even possible?"

It had only been three months since the lights went out, but it seemed like years since Savanah had been able to flick a switch and the lights come on. The mere thought of taking a hot shower sent her into giddy laughter.

"I'm looking forward to drinking a real cup of coffee," Pete said.

"You think they have coffee?" Isabella asked.

"The medic said they did. Bacon and powdered eggs too."

It was all too good to be true. Savanah knew that Will was reluctant to remain at the shelter and had plans to leave there as soon as they could find a suitable new home, but Savanah was stil hopeful that the army would push the Chinese out of Louisiana, so she could return to her farm. As excited as she was about electricity and bacon, she already missed her home. Winter would be coming soon, and Arkansas was a lot colder than southern Louisiana. It would be months before they could plant anything there and even longer before they could harvest food to put on the table. Going home was all she really wanted. She needed to hold on to that hope. In the meantime, she sure was looking forward to bacon.

THIRTY

Will

Event + Three Months

Will held Isabella's hand as they waited in the long line at the military checkpoint. Razor wire prevented anyone from bypassing it, although, it didn't look like they were turning anyone away. Children cried, and some weary travelers took seats on the road. Every muscle in Will's body hurt. He was looking forward to a warm meal and a cot to rest on.

"They're making people register for the draft," a middle-aged man in front of Will whispered.

Will didn't doubt it. He'd seen the fighting firsthand. They needed more soldiers to make sure that the Chinese never got a foothold on American soil again and he knew that he would likely be one of those drafted. He'd like to get his family settled somewhere, and then he'd consider volunteering. Isabella and Savanah would be furious, but he had a duty to his country. If people like him didn't step up to defend it and rebuild her. Who would? It was his duty.

The line inched forward, and eventually, he stood before the registration desk himself.

"Do you have any identification?" the soldier asked.

Will instinctually touched his right back pocket where he normally kept a wallet. It wasn't there. At this point, he couldn't even recall what had happened to it. It could have been inside the Jeep when they were carjacked.

"No."

"What's your name?"

He gave the soldier all his information, including the names of the relatives with him. He listed Isabella as his wife, just in case they were keeping families together. He didn't want to be separated from her.

"My son is thirteen. We will be able to stay together, right?"

The soldier didn't answer him. A knot formed in Will's stomach. They'd been through so much already. They needed to remain together.

"Hold out your hand," the soldier said.

Will extended his arm toward him. The soldier placed a white plastic band around Will's wrist and pointed to the next table. "You'll get your unit assignment there."

Will's heart sank. "What?" Was he drafted right there? Would they force him to leave his family and whisk him off to the front lines?

"Move along," the soldier said sternly.

When Will didn't comply, the soldier gestured to the military police standing nearby. The two MPs marched over and took Will by the arm. "He said to move on to the next station."

"I need to register my son and my wife," Will said, pointing over his shoulder at them.

"You can do so at the next station. You'll receive your living assignments there."

"What was it I just registered for then?"

"The Selective Service System."

"The draft?" Will asked.

"Yes. Now, move along. We have a lot of people behind you."

Will moved forward and held out his hand to Isabella.

"Ma'am. You'll need to register as well."

"What?" Will asked, his voice pitching high.

"Everyone over the age of eighteen must register," the soldier seated behind the table said.

Will and Isabella looked at one another. She shrugged and stepped up to the table.

"Isabella Fontenot. I'm thirty-two years old and married to him." She pointed to Will and smiled.

Will smiled back. There weren't married yet, but there was no way from FEMA to know that. After all they'd been through, he was determined to make it official though—as soon as possible. He felt like the luckiest man alive. He was so blessed to have found someone as kind and loving as Isabella. He fought back the fear that crept up his spine that they'd both be called up and sent to separate places.

After receiving the living assignments, they were led to a gathering of tents near the back of the sprawling compound and given bedrolls and toiletries. Will stared at the bar of soap. "Does this mean you have running water?"

"We have assigned shower days. With this many people, we have to keep to a schedule."

Isabella's eyes lit up. "Shower! Oh my God!"

Savanah, Jason, and the kids were housed across from them and two tents down with other families with small children. There was a door that locked to protect the little ones. Will had no idea how they could possibly screen the refugees. How many criminals could be among them, and they'd have no way of knowing but Will was sure that Savanah and Jason would keep their children close. He intended to keep a watchful eye on Cayden.

~

Texarkana Refugee Center
One Week Later

It had been a week or more since he'd last seen Pete and his family. They'd been housed in another part of the camp. Will had spotted him in a crowd of people who'd gathered around a radio and politely pushed his way over to him, stopping still when he heard the radio announcer mention the president.

"President Latham will address the nation this evening. According to his press secretary, he will lay out his plan for the nation's recovery."

"Latham?" Will asked.

"Congressmen Latham is now the president," Pete said.

"How'd that happen? Did they have an election I didn't hear about?"

"Sort of, I guess. I was told that he was in the line of succession."

Will took in the information and tried to make sense of it. He hadn't been a very good student when it came to the American government. Line of succession reminded him of a monarchy. They were a republic. They held elections, and the people voted on their president.

"So that means that the rest of the government is gone then?" Will asked.

Pete gestured toward the radio. "It appears so. Latham is supposed to explain all that tonight."

"Have you heard anything about the draft? Are they sending people out yet?"

"Some. People who've been here a little while. Not the newcomers. I heard that soldiers are being sent to shore up the West Coast as well, and there seems to be some trouble up north in the Chicago area. Some general has gone rogue."

"So we could be sent anywhere."

"Just about. After sitting around here for weeks, I'm ready. I don't want to leave my family, but hanging out here just waiting for it is too much."

"I want to get my family settled somewhere first. Jason agrees. The showers and modern amenities are nice, but no one wants to stay here forever."

"They'll be moving people to Houston, Dallas, Austin, and San Antonio soon, I hear. They are working on getting the electric grid back up, and then the camp will be closed."

"How soon will that take place?"

The man next to Pete turned around. "They have power in Austin. That's where the president will set up his office."

Will's eyes widened. They'd made significant progress then. It might only be a matter of months and they could be back to some form of a new normal. Except they'd still be at war and be deployed to the front lines. What would happen to Cayden? Surely they wouldn't send Savanah. She had four kids. Cayden could stay with her if he and Isabella got called up at the same time.

"I need to talk to Jason and Walker. They'll want to hear the president's speech."

~

Texarkana Refugee Center
Event + Four Months

A month after hearing President Latham lay out his plan to rebuild the nation's power grid and provide essential services to the people who had survived the nightmare, Will, Pete, Walker, and Jason found themselves enlisted in the Texas National Guard. Pete said that their basic training was a joke. Will was glad. His tired body couldn't have survived doing push-ups anymore, and the four a.m. road marches were torture on his knees.

Their first post was to be an airport in Little Rock, Arkansas. It was far from the fighting out on the West Coast and the tedious and boring postings down along the gulf coast not that he'd have minded sitting on Galveston Beach watching the waves now that the Navy had cleared the gulf of enemy ships and submarines. Isabella might still have that pleasure. She had yet to learn of her duty station. Savanah was exempt, and she would remain with the children, including Cayden.

Will still had plans to use his free time to scout for a permanent home for them, someplace away from cities. Everyone else would flock there as the lights came back on. The plan to restore power didn't extend to the rural areas—not yet. It could be years before electricity flowed in rural Arkansas and Will was actually looking forward to getting back to that simpler way of life—not the hunger, but the self-sufficient lifestyle.

A week before they were to leave for Little Rock, Savanah and Jason were married by the camp chaplain in a Catholic ceremony. A day later, he and Isabella stood before the same chaplain under a willow tree in a nearby park. Cayden was his best man. The smile on his face when he handed Will the ring said it all. He'd given them his blessing when Will had approached him about asking Isabella to marry him, but Will had held on to doubt until that moment. Cayden adored Isabella, and she loved him like her own. Will thought of Melanie on their wedding day. She would be so proud of her son. Will knew that she wanted them to move on and be happy.

Will had traded his toiletries to a guy running a black market just outside the camp for a simple wedding band. As he slid the band onto Isabella's finger, he stared into her tear-filled eyes. They were tears of joy. After all they'd been through over the last five months, they deserved this little bit of happiness.

"You may now kiss the bride," the chaplain said.

Will took Isabella into his arms and kissed her tenderly. He didn't want this moment to end. It was the most content he'd been in a very long time.

"Get a room!" Pete called out.

Isabella laughed, and Will released her. He took her hand, and they marched back down the aisle between their friends. They'd found a room for their honeymoon. They'd spend the night in a former old Victorian bed and breakfast. The owners were gone, and they'd be bringing their own breakfast, but that was exactly how Will wanted it. He'd had very little time alone with Isabella since they'd met and was ecstatic to have her all to himself, even if it were only for one night.

They tried their best not to talk about what the future looked like. Each knew that there was no way to predict. They had this together, and one thing Will had learned for certain was that he had to cherish every moment. No one was promised a tomorrow.

Thank you for purchasing No Surrender, book four in the Fall of Houston series. **The story continues in book five, No Man's Land. Pre-order the ebook version on Amazon.com today!**

Have you read my Days of Want series? If not, please check it out by visiting Amazon.com and order your copy today.

If you enjoyed No Surrender, I'd like to hear from you and hope that you could take a moment and post an honest review on Amazon. Your support and feedback will help this author improve for future projects. Without the support of readers like yourself, self-publishing would not be possible.

Don't forget to sign up for my spam-free newsletter at tlpayne.com to be the first to know of new releases, giveaways and special offers.

No Surrender has gone through several layers of editing. If you found a typographical, grammatical, or other error which impacted your enjoyment of the book, I offer my apologies and ask that you let me know so I can fix it for future readers. To do so, click here to fill out the form or email me at contact@tlpayne.com. In appreciation, I would like to offer you a free copy of my next book.

Also by T. L. Payne

Fall of Houston Series

No Way Out

No Other Choice

No Turning Back

No Surrender

No Man's Land (Pre-Order Now!)

The Days of Want Series

Turbulent

Hunted

Turmoil

Uprising

Upheaval

Mayhem

Defiance (Coming Summer 2021!)

The Gateway to Chaos Series

Seeking Safety

Seeking Refuge

Seeking Justice

Seeking Hope

Seeking Sanctuary (Coming Soon!)

About the Author

T. L. Payne is the author of the bestselling Days of Want, Gateway to Chaos, and Fall of Houston series. T. L. lives and writes in the Osage Hills region of Oklahoma and enjoys many outdoor activities including kayaking, rockhounding, metal detecting, and fishing the many lakes and rivers of the area.

Don't forget to sign up for T. L.'s spam-free newsletter at www.tlpayne.com to be the first to know of new releases, giveaways and special offers.

T. L. loves to hear from readers. You may email T. L. at contact@tlpayne.com or join the Facebook reader group at https://www.facebook.com/groups/tlpaynereadergroup

Made in the USA
Coppell, TX
17 June 2021